The

XIII

a novel
by
Kat Yares

This book is dedicated to my wonderful husband, Kevin, who constantly gives his undying support to my stories. Without him, none would ever be written.

I must also thank CBS Sunday Morning for the spark that generated the story line and current news from certain companies that made me realize that now was the time to publish The XIII.

The XIII is a work of fiction. All characters, situations and locations came from the authors own twisted mind. Any and all similarity to real people and places is purely coincidental.

Prologue

The carpenter worked slowly, but expertly as he fitted the light colored wood into the recessed wood of the deep brown tabletop. With his skill for woodworking, no nails would be needed to hold the inlay in place. He stepped back to look at his handiwork. Each of the thirteen points of the star was perfect in every way.

From behind him, he heard the door open and watched as a red-haired man approached.

"Judas, my friend. What brings you here?"

"The imposter from Tarsus is still in Jerusalem spreading his lies."

"Peter hangs on his every word, he sees personal glory in them."

"What should I do, master?"

"Kill him."

The Year of Our Lord, sixty-nine years after his birth.

Thirteen men sat around the star imbedded table. The table and the men themselves had relocated from Glastonbury to Rome several years prior.

"The Jews in Jerusalem are out of control." The son of Judas explained to the others. "They spread lies and cause persecution to both us and our families."

The son of Yahshua sat back quietly and listened. Looking at a young blond haired man across the table, he said,

"You will go to Caesar. It is time to fulfill the prophesy of my father."

"I will do as you say, master." The son of Peter replied.

Two weeks later, Jerusalem was nothing more than burning rubble.

The destruction of Rome

Three hundred years passed before the descendants of the thirteen felt they must make their presence known again. Now located in Constantinople, the thirteen men met at the table hidden in a room within the temple dome.

"The empire is losing ground fast. Constantly it loses land and holdings." The man in the white robe stood. "It is time for a change in the world. Any suggestions?"

"Lord Constantine is very loved by the people. He follows our words; he would make a great leader." The man wearing the purple robe said solemnly.

Every man seated around the star table nodded their agreement.

The white robed man responded, "You have made a wise choice, son of Peter." He looked to the other men. "Make it so."

The first Pope

Ten years later, the group met again, this time back in Rome.

"We need a spiritual guide to lead the masses. One educated in our ways."

"Felix has trained and studied with the son of Nathan for years. He has served both the sons of Matthew and Bartholomew well. He would be a good choice." The man in the purple robe offers the solution once again.

"Will the people accept him?" The man in white asked.

"They will accept him." The man in red responded, his voice almost defiant.

Seeing the agreement among the others, the man in the white robe stood and said, "Make it so."

The Crusades

Centuries had passed and still the thirteen met yearly at the star table. Having come together once more, the man in the white robe said,

"These followers of the heretic Mohammed are a threat. To us, to the civilized world, to the masses."

"We must eradicate them," the man in the purple robe said.

"That is our goal," the man in the green robe answered, "The question is the how of the situation."

"The how is simple, we send out a battle cry to the entirety of the Christian world. We call for the heads of these heretics that would destroy Christianity."

"A brilliant plan, son of Peter." The man in the white robe said. "It shall be funded by the church; all god-fearing men will fight the heretics in order to wipe them from the face of the earth."

The Roman Inquisition

The year of our lord, 1226 A.D.

The men gathered around the star table. No longer wearing the robes of their ancestors, they now wore the clothing of the French court.

3

"The masses are rebelling and the aristocracy is refusing to pay tithes." The man dressed in emerald green velvet said.

"We have come together to find an answer to this problem. The king is totally ineffectual." The man wearing white velvet added.

As in ages past, the man wearing purple supplied the answer, "We have the King publicly tortured and execute the offenders. That would stop any further uprisings."

Each man at the round table nodded his agreement. Turning to the man in red, the leader said, "Take our solution to Honorius III, I am sure you will receive the Pope's full cooperation."

The Spanish Inquisition

Two hundred years later in a converted mosque outside Madrid, the thirteen men once more came to the table.

"King Ferdinand and Queen Isabella have lost control of the Spanish empire. The Jews and the Protestants are slowly, but completely taking over not only trade but also the royal court."

"We must send to Rome," the man directly across the table from the leader said. "We must begin another inquisition, all heretics must die."

Around the room, each man nodded his agreement.

"Tell the king and queen what must be done." The leader said to the man sitting at his side.

The American Revolution

The star table was once again circled by the thirteen men. As one man rose, the others looked to him in expectation.

"Gentlemen, we have the opportunity to shape a country. A country more than ever before will bend and bow to our wishes. The colonists are dissatisfied with their mother country and the aristocracy is greedy. By allowing each to think the other will serve their needs, we can force the separation of one country from another."

The man looked around the room, seeing both quizzical looks and nods of appreciation. He continued,

"Once the first goal has been achieved, then it will be nothing to put puppets into power. From that moment on, we will pull the strings on these marionettes and the world will be ours. Are we in agreement?"

To each man, the leader turned and was greeted by nods of the head.

"Then let us work out a plan." he said smiling as he sat down to his place at the table.

World War One

Thirteen men sat around the star table located in a remote castle deep in the Prussian wilderness.

"Gentlemen, the world has once again become chaotic. The masses are rebelling, much as they did during the two revolutions. It is time to take action."

"And your suggestion would be?"

"We need to reduce the population once more. Only by war will we do that effectively." came the reply.

"But how to start it?"

"An assassination would be a good start."

"Who do you suggest?"

Archduke Ferdinand. War between Prussia and England afterwards. The world will come together to fight this war."

"I will find our assassin." said the man next to the speaker.

"Make it so."

5

The star table had traveled a great journey once more. Now located deep within the Colorado Mountains, its thirteen members sat and discussed how to bring the United States into the conflict happening in Europe.

"I had thought they would come to England's aide." one man said.

"We miscalculated on this president — I too thought he would come to the aide of the motherland. We need something more drastic."

"America needs to be attacked on its own shores." said another.

"Germany is overstretched as it is — they do not have the resources to come this far from home." yet another man said.

"Japan." the man next to the leader said simply, "I can convince Japan to bomb the harbor in Hawaii."

The thirteen men in the room nodded their approval.

"Make it so." the leader said.

Chapter One

The deep amber shades of sunset radiated from the horizon of the tall white peaked mountains down on the snakelike highway below. The rays glared off the sleek, shiny black Jaguar as it sped, top down, hugging the tiny sliver of roadway. Inside the Jag, Alicia Benedict attempted to hold the wheel with one hand as her other fished the floorboard for her dropped cell phone. Her very pregnant belly and the closeness of the steering wheel made the search more difficult. Every few moments, her dark ebony face would lose its beauty as another labor pain soared through her otherwise lithe body.

She unfastened the seat belt for more maneuverability and leaned over as she felt the tip of the phone under her right foot. Taking her foot from the gas momentarily, she scooted the phone back within reach. The speedometer read ninety-five as her fingers gripped the phone and she looked up just in time to see the curve. Yet, not quickly enough to react as the wheels of the Jag left the pavement and the car soared over the unprotected mountain embankment. Her last conscious thought was to press the emergency button on the cell phone, then her head hit the steering wheel. She passed out for the remainder of the hundred-foot slide down the mountain.

***

Patrick Benedict stormed into the hospital emergency lobby. "My wife, where is she?" his deep voice echoed throughout the floor. He advanced toward the counter as people scrambled to get out of his way.

Several were not able to move quickly enough, and were pushed aside by the big man.

From behind the swinging doors of a hallway, a man emerged and gripped Patrick by the arm.

"Patrick, you must calm down. They are doing all they can."

"Where is she?"

"She's down the hall, in one of the emergency rooms. She's in bad shape, Pat."

"The baby? Is it still alive?"

"I don't know, Pat. They've been working since she was brought in. They haven't said anything yet.'

"What do you mean, they have told you nothing? For Christ's sake, Adam, you're her bother." Patrick's anger was rising, his face flushed with a redness that almost matched his hair.

He pushed Adam aside and stormed through the double doors down the hallway. He paused long enough to look into each room as he passed. In the next to the last room, he saw his wife's battered face through the glass. He entered the room.

Several nurses rushed to push him out, but he stood his ground. Around his wife, several doctors blocked his view.

"I demand to know what is going on." his voice resonated off the walls as he walked closer to the bedside.

"Sir, you can't be in here." one of the doctors said, never looking up from his patient.

"That is my wife. And I will be here. How bad is it?"

"Sir, we are doing our best to save both your wife and child. If you will wait outside, someone will bring you news." the young doctor said.

"I will wait right here." he answered as he reached for his wife's hand.

"Call security; get this man out of here." one doctor said to a nearby nurse.

"Yes, Doctor," the nurse replied as she pressed a button mounted on the wall.

Looking over at the monitors, Patrick could see that her heartbeat was very weak. The monitor attached to the child showed a beat that seemed stronger, yet obviously distressed.

"Save the child." he said, as he stroked Alicia's cheek.

"Sir we're doing all we can." another doctor responded.

"Save the child. Do what you must, but save the child." Patrick stared at the doctor causing the other man to look away.

"We're losing her..." a voice came from the other side of the table.

Patrick looked up at the heart monitor and saw that the beat had flat-lined. His eyes shifted back to the baby monitor.

Turning to look again at his dead wife, he said quietly, "I'm sorry Alicia."

Moments later, he heard the first cry of his child. Turning to the end of the gurney, he looked as the doctor held the child with the umbilical cord attached toward him.

"You have a beautiful baby girl." the doctor said.

Patrick Benedict turned back to his wife, stoking her cheek and for an immediate instant, his expression softened. "I did love you, you know? Good bye, Alicia."

He laid her hand back across her chest, and turned and started for the door.

Two security guards entered the room and took him by each arm. Patrick shrugged them off as the doctor gave a signal that it was all right.

"I'm leaving." Patrick said simply.

"Sir, would you like to hold your daughter?" one of the nurses asked.

Without turning around or missing a step, he replied,

"They told us it was a boy."

Chapter Two

Olga Swenson sat in the rocker holding the small baby girl in her arms. As she looked down at the child, she could not hide the pity on her face. The mother had died from injuries received in the car accident that had forced this child's birth three weeks early. The father, on learning the child was a girl and not the boy they had been told, had walked out of the room and had never looked at the child.

Earlier that morning, Olga had learned that an adoption agency was picking up the child later in the afternoon. The child, named only Baby Benedict, would need to be ready for pickup by two p.m. As she rocked the baby, she wondered how anyone could give up such a child. The talk for weeks around the nursery had been of Patrick Benedict, his money and his callousness.

Olga heard a noise from the front desk. A stern looking woman, hair drawn tightly into a bun, stood on the other side handing papers to the head nurse, Sabine Ferguson. Looking first at the clock and then down at the baby, Olga sighed and whispered,

"I guess it's that time, pretty girl. How I hope that your new parents are better than the father you have. Hopefully you'll never know how heartlessly you have been thrown away."

She stood as Sabine nodded her head. Wrapping the quilt from her lap around the baby, she began walking toward the front desk. Sabine took the child from her arms and handed her to the woman.

"You will find her a good home?" Sabine asked.

"We already have it picked out. The child will have the best of everything." the woman answered, not yet looking down at the baby in her arms.

11

"That's good then." Sabine said.

Without another word, the woman turned and began her walk toward the elevator. Olga looked at Sabine.

"It just seems so wrong," she said, shaking her head.

"The rich and powerful, they have a different way of doing things." Sabine replied.

"Then I'll stay poor. I could never abandon a child like that."

"Neither could I, but you know what they say, what goes around comes around. I'm sure Mr. Benedict will get his someday." Sabine smiled.

"Wonder if today would be too soon?" Olga asked, herself grinning.

***

The reception was small, only the twelve men and their wives witnessed the marriage of Patrick Benedict to Ariel Edwards three months after the death of his wife Alicia and the birth of his girl child. Looking at Ariel, the spitting image of her twin Alicia, it was as if Alicia had never died at all.

Joseph Christianson walked over and patted Patrick on the back.

"I knew you would remarry soon, but this was rather unexpected." he said to his long time friend.

"What can I say? Ariel is pregnant." Patrick replied.

"Pregnant? How did that happen?" Joseph asked.

"The usual way." the groom answered with a smile. "She stayed after Alicia's funeral. We got drunk... things happened."

"What did you tell her about the child?" Joseph asked quickly.

12

"That she had died with her mother." Patrick answered.

"She asked no other questions?"

"No, I just told her the child was buried in the coffin with her mother. She thought that was sweet. Made her even more sympathetic to me."

"So have you confirmed the sex of this child?" Joseph asked.

"They did an amino yesterday, confirmed it was a boy."

"Three months along? Then your son should be here the within a month of mine. Murial is four months along now... it too is a boy."

"Well congratulations to you also, then Joseph. We truly have much to celebrate this day." the red haired man said, nodding with a smile.

"That we do Patrick, that we do."

Chapter Three

Murial Christianson felt no pain as she lay on the birthing room table. The drug, being fed into her blood stream intravenously took care of that. Around her, she was surrounded by the best medical team that money could buy. Good private doctors and nurses, the comfort of her own nursery, complete with a neo-natal unit in case of problems and her husband standing at her side to insure that nothing dared go wrong. So far, she had not even mussed her perfectly coifed blond hair.

"I should have had a caesarian." she said calmly to her husband, Joseph.

Standing well over six foot, Joe had to bend over to whisper in her ear, "You didn't want a scar, remember?"

Murial smiled. A scar didn't seem so bad now, but this time next year, she would want to be relaxing on the beach in her bikini.

"Ok, Murial, you're going to have to push a bit now." the doctor standing between her legs said from behind his mask.

"See, it's almost over." Joe said smiling.

"I thought I wasn't supposed to feel anything?" Murial said as her eyebrows arched.

"It's just pressure... not pain."

"And how would you know that?" Murial responded, as her hands white knuckled the holding bars on the sides of the bed.

"Once more, should do it." The doctor said, ignoring her previous comment.

"Push, ma'am. We're real close now." the nurse by her side said.

Murial scrunched up her face and pushed with all her strength. She felt like she was being ripped apart and then just as suddenly the sensation passed. She heard a cry.

"It's a boy!" the doctor said holding out the child for her to see. "Would you like to hold him, while I finish up here?"

For a moment, Murial was repulsed by the small red body that was laid across her upper body, but within seconds her maternal instincts kicked in and she reached down and pulled the child closer to her face.

"You did it, Murial. He's beautiful." Joseph said quietly.

"Our son." she whispered, tears streaming down her face.

"Joshua Joseph Christianson, the fifth."

Murial looked up at her husband. His face beamed with the pride that she felt also.

Chapter Four

Joseph Christianson stood proudly beaming at the twelve men who sat at the massive round mahogany table with its inlay of teak in thirteen even sections forming a perfect thirteen-pointed star. As Joe, handed out cigars wrapped in blue paper, he said,

"Gentlemen, a new generation has begun."

Around him, the other twelve men nodded, smiled and offered congratulations. A butler entered the room pushing a cart holding four silver champagne buckets. Two servants entered behind him carrying champagne glasses on trays. The butler uncorked the bottles and the crystal glasses were filled and placed in front of each man. When the last was in place, Patrick Benedict rose from his chair.

"May I suggest a toast?" he asked in a loud booming voice. "To Joshua Joseph Christianson, the fifth. May his life be blessed and may he fulfill all our hopes and dreams."

"Hear, hear!" the others boomed as Patrick raised his glass and tapped the goblet Joseph was holding. Each man in his turn, rose and did the same.

The glasses drained, Joseph continued to stand.

"Gentlemen, we have made some mistakes in the past. I am sure I do not need to remind any of us of that. The labs have brought good news. The genetic restructuring we have done on apple seeds seem to be having the desired effect. They ask for another year of testing, before they will allow human testing. Is that satisfactory with everyone?"

"Tell them to make it five. We have to be sure this time, Joe." Payton Stone, sitting a half table away from him, said.

"That is too long." Johann Carpenter said from directly across.

"A compromise gentlemen, three years. Then we will begin testing in Ethiopia. If all works out as planned, we can advance to all of Africa within twenty years." Joseph said quickly.

"Three years, I can accept that." Thomas Fisher replied.

"I can also," responded Johann.

"Gentlemen, by the time my son reaches age to take over, we will have eliminated hunger in this world." Joseph beamed with pride.

"Agreed." said several around the table.

"As an aside, Patrick, I think congratulations for you will soon be in order. I understand Ariel is due to deliver in a few days also?"

"She is due in a week." Patrick said. "This time, all the tests say it is a boy. I do not think I could handle the disappointment again."

"You will not be." Joseph said. "Payton, it is time you married also."

"Haven't found the right woman." Payton replied.

"Right woman? Hell man, any woman with the right breeding is right." Joseph's voice grew cold. "Marry June, she will do."

"I don't love her." Payton said.

"Love has nothing to do with it. You are already behind."

"But.."

"But nothing." Joseph said. "Marry her in the spring. Women like that. Get her pregnant. You can always keep another on the side for fun."

"Joseph..."

"All in favor of Payton marrying June come spring, raise their hands."

Around the table, eleven hands were raised.

"Motion carried. You have your task." Joseph said, his eyes burning into Payton's.

Payton stared back as Joseph continued, "The rest of you, well...you will have your congratulations within the year."

Chapter Five

Payton Stone, III stood on the steps of Ashleigh Preparatory School tears streaming down his face watching his father's limousine pull away from the school. Although he tried to be a big boy, at five years old, the thought that he would never see his mother again overwhelmed him. The headmaster stood at his side, holding his hand, yet when the tears would not stop, he said sternly,

"Mr. Stone, you will not behave as a baby here at Ashleigh." the man stooped and put his face inches from the child's, "You will stop your sobbing and behave like a man. Like your father."

Payton looked at the man and fear stopped the tears much faster than they had started. The man's grip on his small hand became tighter.

"We are always men here at Ashleigh, young Mr. Stone. You will be no exception."

Payton looked out into the side yard, watching other boys play soccer.

"Come now, Mr. Carlisle will show you to your dorm room. You will meet your room mates just before dinner."

Payton felt himself being pulled along though the massive doors of the school. Inside the doors, his hand was given to a man whose face, to the young child, resembled an eagle.

"Mr. Carlisle, will you see to it that Mr. Stone is settled into his dorm room. And ask Mr. Christianson to be sure to watch out for him."

"Yes sir." Carlisle responded.

"And, Carlisle," the headmaster continued, "tell Mr. Benedict to make a man out of him."

"Yes sir." the older man replied.

Five hours later, his clothing and personal possessions put away by Mr. Carlisle, Payton sat on his bed, tears long since spent as twelve other boys entered the room.

"Finally, we are now thirteen. Welcome, Payton." a good-looking boy of about eight said.

"Who are you?"

"Josh Christianson." the older boy smiled. "And this is Julian, and Tom, and Andy and John." he said pointing to each boy in turn. After he had finished naming each, he said,

"We are your roommates for the next nine or ten years."

"Ten years?" Payton asked, a quiver returning to his voice.

"You bet." Josh said. "We are brothers from here on out. We are your family."

"I already have a family." Payton said.

"You'll see, in a few weeks you won't even miss them."

As the weeks passed, Payton fell into the routine of the school. Josh had been right as the days went by he missed his parents less and less. Although younger than the rest of the boys by about three years, they made sure to include him in most of their activities. But in classes, he was alone. Bright as he was, it was in the different classes that he felt the most abandoned. The other kids ignored him and several times already he had caught them talking and laughing about him behind his back. Josh told him to ignore them, Julian said he would take care of it in its time.

The weeks turned into months and as Julian promised, his other classmates no longer laughed at or made fun of him. Instead, they ignored him totally, going out of their way not to talk to him. Other than his twelve roommates, he had no friends of his own and everyday as he sat in the classroom, he paid more attention to the clock than to the teacher.

Christmas approached, Payton assumed that his father would be coming to get him for the holidays. His classmates all bragged about their plans for the vacation and he looked forward to going home.

"Josh, when do you think my dad will be here?" he finally asked one night after classes.

"Payton, I told you-we're your family now. We stay here for the holidays."

"But.."

"Oh, don't worry. They'll send you tons of presents. That's what matters the most, right? And they'll have a great tree here, and parties, plus we can do what we want."

"Will I never see my mom and dad again?" Payton was near tears.

"Oh you'll see them again, don't sweat it. But not till summer and then it's only for a short time. We'll all go to camp together and then it will be back here in the fall."

Payton felt more miserable than he had on his first day. He looked at Julian, whose face dared him to cry. Taking a deep breath, he curled up on his bed, drawing his knees into his chest and put on a brave face. The other's returned to what they were doing, yet every once in a while, Payton would catch either Josh or Julian stealing a glance at him. Josh he did not mind, although he was jealous of the way everyone seemed to do exactly what he wanted. But Julian terrified him for reasons he could not explain. Maybe it was the bright red hair, or maybe his loud voice, but of all the others in the room, Julian was the one that Payton wished was not there at all.

***

At nine years old, Maria Sanchez was already showing the beauty she would become at adulthood. Her long, dark auburn hair had just enough curl to insure she would never have to perm it and perfectly set off her light coffee colored skin and emerald green eyes. As her mother brushed her hair, she finally worked up the courage to ask the question that had been bothering her for weeks.

"Mom, do you know who my real parents are?"

As soon as the question was out of her mouth, she regretted asking as she saw her mother's expression in the mirror in front of her. Her mother's expression quickly softened as she answered,

"No honey we don't."

Maria fidgeted in the chair, wanting to ask more but very unsure if she dared.

"We have had you since you were three week old, baby. We were told your mother died in an auto accident. They told us nothing about your father."

Like the daughter, the mother watched her child's expression in the mirror, knowing there were more questions to follow.

"Honey, you can ask anything you want. Whatever we know, we will tell you."

"Thanks, Mama." the young girl replied. "So how did you get me?"

"Your father and I tried for many years to have a baby. After we had been to a lot of doctors, we found out that we couldn't. But we still wanted a child to call our own. So we went to several adoption agencies. After waiting a long, long time, they finally called us and told us about you. We hurried to the hospital and right outside the door, they handed you to us. It was the happiest day of our lives. We finally had our baby, our little girl."

22

Carlita Sanchez laid the brush on the vanity and stooped down beside her daughter's chair. Pulling her close with both arms, she held her tight against her chest.

"It never mattered to us that we weren't your birth parents. We loved you the moment we saw you. We could have never had a daughter as beautiful and wonderful as you. Do you understand what I am saying? You are our perfect child."

"I understand, Mama. You are the perfect mom, too." Maria smiled. "But one more question, Mama. Will the adoption agency tell me who my real parents were?"

Carlita smiled, she knew this day was coming and had dreaded it, yet was prepared.

"When you are all grown up, then yes, I think they will have to tell you more. But not until then. Until then honey, you can ask us anything. Your dad and I will do our best to help you with the answers to your questions. Okay?"

"Okay, Mama." the little girl replied. "So where are we going for dinner?" she asked, her mind awhirl, knowing that someday she would find out just who she really was.

Chapter Six

For reasons Payton couldn't understand, Josh had been secretive all week. It was the last of September and they had only been back on campus for little over two weeks. Payton knew, today the twenty-ninth was Josh's thirteenth birthday and had enlisted old Carlisle's help in getting Josh a present. As they dressed for classes in the matching uniforms, Payton noticed that Josh selected a different jacket and pants than the required dress from his closet.

"You're going to be in real trouble if you wear that, Josh." Payton said, his voice almost panicky.

"I am not going to classes today. I get to fly to ENKI."

"You're going to ENKI?" Payton's voice raised a pitch. "But how, I didn't think we could go there until we are grown up."

"We are grown up. The minute we turn thirteen. We become men. At least that is what my father says." Josh winked at Payton.

"But what about your party? We always have our birthday parties here." the younger boy couldn't keep the whine out of his voice.

"We will party later. I mean, come on, Payton, I get to see ENKI Headquarters."

"I know, but..."

"No buts, I have heard about this place for years, but I have never known where it was. Today I get to see it." excitement was building in Josh's voice.

"I know all that. I want to see it too. After all, our fathers own it. But, still..."

"Like I said, no buts. I will tell you guys all about it when I get back."

"What about your presents and stuff?"

24

"We'll do that when I get back too. Okay?"

"Okay." Payton said, disappointment dripping in his voice.

Payton waited all day for Josh's return. When he finally returned the next day, he would tell Payton, nor the others, anything more than ENKI was beautiful. He refused to tell them what had happened there, only promising they would learn on their birthdays.

Payton could see the excitement fill the other boy's faces. Julian would be thirteen next week, and each of them except Payton would be thirteen within the next seven months. Payton had three years to wait.

Chapter Seven

The thirteen boys stood together in the corner of the large gymnasium. All wore the traditional black tuxedo required for all school dances, all looked bored. Josh held a crystal cup filled with punch, the others had platefuls of various finger sandwiches and other appetizers.

"At least this is the last time I'll have to do this." Josh said. At sixteen, he would be a senior next year and these events would no longer be mandatory for him and several of the others including Julian.

"It's not so bad. At least we get to see what the girls look like out of their uniforms." Julian said grinning. "Most times you can't see the curves, but here... ah... and those curves are nice in silk and satin."

"How long do we have to stay?" Payton asked, feeling more uncomfortable by the minute.

"Till it is over, I suppose." Julian replied.

"This is terribly boring." Thomas said, looking up, the ceiling tiles obviously more interesting than the dance happening in front of him.

"Whoa, now who is that?" Josh asked, pointing at a young girl of about seventeen who had just entered the gym.

The new arrival, along with four or five other girls, stood just inside the entry. The light from the mirrored ball suspended from the ceiling flashed highlights on her long, wavy auburn hair. The cream-colored formal gown was cut low over her breasts, clung sensuously to her hips, and tightened down her legs. Even in the dim light, the cream of the dress set off her coffee colored skin.

"I don't know, but I'd like to." Julian said quickly, his eyes lighting up, as he caught site of the young woman.

"She reminds me a bit of you." Payton said. "What with that red hair and dark skin."

Julian smiled. "Must mean, she's just my type." he said as he sat his plate down on a nearby table.

"I saw her first." Josh said. He laughed as he laid his drink down and began walking across the floor toward her.

"She is pretty, isn't she?" Thomas asked Payton as they watched Josh approach her.

"She's a goddess." Julian said. "I mean, just look at her. Beauty and a body to die for."

Payton blushed. He hated times like this when his younger age was even more evident. The other boys at sixteen had already begun dating. At not quite thirteen, he was considered too young. It had only been because of the others insistence that he had been allowed to attend the dance, normally he wouldn't have been permitted to attend for another two years.

"She's okay, I guess." he said.

"Okay?" Julian said, shock sounding in his voice. "My dear little brother, you have much to learn." He patted Payton on the back. "Me, I'm going to go see if Josh is getting anywhere. Hopefully not."

Payton and the others watched as Julian joined Josh at the young woman's side. From his viewpoint, it didn't appear to Payton either of them was getting anywhere at all. Yet when the orchestra began a slow melody, Josh swept the girl into his arms and began a slow dance. Payton could see that Julian wished he had thought of it first.

Julian walked back to the other boys. "Have you ever seen anything like her? I swear she must be an angel."

"So does this angel have a name?" Thomas asked.

"Maria something or other." Julian replied.

"Too blinded by her beauty to pay attention to what she said?" Andrew looked at Julian and smiled.

"Maybe." Julian said with a shrug, "Or maybe she didn't say."

"You going to try and get the next dance?" Andrew asked.

"Plan to." Julian's head nodded in affirmation, "Plan on cutting in on Josh before this song is done, just to make sure." he smiled.

"Wish I had your nerve." Thomas said.

"I still don't get it. She's just a girl. Besides if you cut in, won't Josh get mad?" Payton said, now wishing he were anywhere but here.

"All fair in love and war, little brother. And I promise, one day soon, you will get it." Julian replied as he started toward the dancing couple.

Chapter Eight

Payton awoke knowing today would be the best day of his young life. Today he turned thirteen and today would be his day to visit ENKI Headquarters. Each of the boys, starting with Josh, had made the trip on their thirteenth birthday, returning with a secret they could only discuss with those who had already made the trip. For almost three years, Payton had been the odd man out, the only one that had not known what they whispered about. Today he would find out.

His father's limo was scheduled to pick him up in less than an hour. Choosing a suit, shirt and tie from the closet, he realized this would also be the first time in years he had not worn a school issued uniform or tuxedo. As he dressed, the others began returning from breakfast.

"Happy Birthday, Payton." Josh said, giving him a big bear hug.

"Ditto on that, Payton." Julian said, hugging him too.

"After tonight, there will be no more secrets between us." Josh said, "You'll truly be one of the thirteen."

"I wish I knew what that meant." Payton said, but not allowing himself to dwell on it. Nothing was going to ruin his mood today.

"You'll see." Josh said, patting him on the back.

The rest of the young men chimed in their congratulations as they entered the room. Payton had just slid his feet into his loafers when Old Carlisle entered the dorm room,

"Master Stone, your car has arrived." he said with a formal bow.

"Guess I should go." Payton turned to the others. "Is it really that big? This thing I'll learn today?"

"It's that big, Payton. It will change your world." Josh replied.

Payton shrugged his shoulders, knowing that none of them would tell him anything more. Grabbing his suit jacket, he turned to follow Old Carlisle to his father's waiting limo.

The limo went only a few miles to what was obviously a private airfield. As the car glided to a halt, Payton saw the ENKI Lear Jet standing ready at the end of the runway. The chauffeur opened the passenger side door of the vehicle,

"Master Stone, your plane awaits." he said with a smile.

Payton climbed from the car and walked quickly to the steps to board the plane. His eyes filled with wonder as he entered the cabin. Thirteen heavily padded leather seats sat in a circle around a large, highly polished, wooden, round table. A huge thirteen-pointed star was inlaid into the table. On the back of each seat was a simple gold plaque engraved with what he assumed were the surnames the other twelve members of ENKI. Payton was surprised to see that the names were identical to those of his dorm roommates. He had thought only his and Josh's fathers owned ENKI. For all these years, he had been certain that the other boy's father's just worked for the company.

From behind a curtain that blended so well with the cabin that he did not notice it, a man emerged.

"If you will take your seat, Master Stone, we will be on our way." the man turned the leather seat with Stone engraved on the back toward him. Payton, still in awe, walked forward and sat down.

"We should be in the air momentarily, sir. Once we are, I'll be back to see if you require anything."

Payton could only nod at the man as he felt the wheels of the jet begin to roll down the runway. Payton had always known that his father was rich, but what he saw as his eyes surveyed the room left him in total shock. One wall of the cabin was fully mirrored and had gold and brass trimmings lining the dark bar that stood in front. The other wall, also mirrored, was lined with bookshelves filled with books that looked very ancient, yet well cared for. A golden rail held them in place. The floor was covered with thick burgundy carpet, and while Payton knew nothing about wood, as he rubbed his hand over the smooth, glossy surface, he knew the table in front of him had to have cost a small fortune.

Payton sat back in the chair. There were no windows for him to look outside, so he continued to look around the cabin, taking in the vast splendor of it all.

The man returned from behind the curtain.

"Would you care for breakfast, sir?"

Payton realized he was indeed hungry. "What are my choices?" he asked.

"What ever you wish sir. And may I say Happy Birthday to you also?"

"Thank you." Payton replied, unsure of what to do next. "Would an omelet be possible?"

"What would you like in that?"

"It's my birthday, surprise me." Payton responded quickly. "Anything but mushrooms." he added.

"Yes, sir. I'll have it ready for you momentarily."

"Thank you." Payton said again.

When his omelet arrived, Payton ate quickly, washing it down with fresh squeezed orange juice. Only when the glass and plate were empty did he realized that they each, along with the silverware, carried the same emblem that was on the table. He assumed it must be the ENKI logo and wondered how much more he didn't know about everything.

The meal had been far better than the food served at school, and better than most restaurants he and the others had ate in, and now bored he wished he had ordered more.

The plane flew for what seemed like hours to Payton. He didn't have a watch so he had no way of knowing just how much time had passed, yet he was already hungry again for the third time. Now he understood why each boy's journey had taken two days to complete. When the man appeared again from behind the curtain, he was about to ask if he could have something else, when the man said,

"We will be landing in a few moments, Master Stone. I'll see you on the return trip."

"Finally." the boy responded, "How far have we gone?"

"That will be up to the others to tell you, sir." the man replied before disappearing behind the curtain.

Minutes later, the cabin door opened and another man stood in the doorway.

"Your car is waiting, sir. Please follow me."

Payton, not knowing what else to do, stood and followed the man. Outside the plane, sand and palm trees were everywhere. Getting into the limo, he watched the landscape go by as he wondered which desert he was in. Within minutes, they pulled through large wrought iron gates supported by massive stone columns.

The limousine came to a stop outside the most beautiful building Payton had ever seen. Reminiscence of an Arabian Mosque, the building looked ancient. A gold plated dome covered what appeared to be the main building confirming Payton's thought that he must be somewhere in the Middle East. On the walls, murals and symbols were carved and painted. The paintings reminded him of artworks he had seen in books of the old Persian Empire.

32

When the chauffeur opened the door, he saw his father walking across the courtyard to meet him.

"Big day, Payton my son."

"Where is this place?" Payton asked, finding it hard to breath in the arid air.

"Outside Jerusalem." his father replied, putting his arm around the boy's shoulder and leading him across the courtyard toward two massive wooden doors.

Entering the building, Payton saw that the walls were lined with tapestries, the floors covered by Persian Rugs and gold and sliver sconces and chandeliers lighted the hallways. Following his father up the stairs, they paused outside wooden double doors with gold handles.

"Son, what you learn here today can never be shared with any man or woman outside the thirteen. Today you become a full member. Never forget the responsibility being placed on you today. Today you become a man."

Payton felt both proud and terrified at the same time. What could be behind these doors, he thought to himself. At the same time, he wondered if what was behind the doors was what had caused his family to abandon him at the boarding school all those years before. He opened his mouth to ask his father, but before he could form the words, his father pushed opened the doors and gently nudged him forward.

As Payton entered the room, the twelve men inside stood and applauded. Payton smiled. He could see resemblances between many of the men and the sons that he knew. Josh was the spitting image of his father. The elder Christianson showed the promise of what Josh would look like in a few years. The only one he couldn't figure out was Julian's father. He had the same red hair, yet not the dark skin of Julian.

One by one, his father took him to meet each man in turn. As they reached Patrick Benedict, the older man could see his confusion. "It's because his mother was black." he said simply. "Haven't they taught you genetics yet?" he smiled.

"No, sir. Next year." Payton replied.

***

Josh and Julian stood to the side of the soccer field watching the others play. As seniors, they no longer had to participate in sports.

"So how's it going with Maria?" Julian asked, hoping for one answer and knowing he would receive another.

"Going well. Can't get in her pants yet, but I will." Josh replied.

"Is that all you think about?" Julian asked.

"Is there anything else?" came the other boy's response.

"Well, when you're finally tired of her turning you down, let me know. I'll treat her right." Julian answered.

"Jude...there's something I've got to tell you about her. I don't know how we both missed it, but I was talking to my father the other day and he told me something quite profound."

"What's that? She's one of us?" Julian asked sarcastically.

"In a way. She's your half-sister, Jude."

"My half-sister? How can that be?" Julian's voice had risen a decibel voicing his disbelief.

"Your father was married before. To your mother's sister. Maria is your father's daughter by her."

"I don't believe that line of shit."

"Ask him. I'm sure he'll tell you."

"Man, I knew you wanted me to stay away from her, but this..." his voice trailed off as he thought about what his best friend had told him. It would explain why

34

she looked so much like him. Payton and several of the others had even commented on it.

"Call your dad, I'm sure he'll explain. And I am sorry, Jude...I was hoping for a little competition."

"I believe you." Julian said knowing that Josh would never lie to him. "But I will ask Dad about it the next time I talk to him." Julian smiled at his friend. "Well now I know she's my sister, you damn well better treat her right." he said with a smile and slugged Josh in the arm.

A week later, as Julian talked to his father and learned all the details of Maria Sanchez, he also learned of another of the Thirteen's big secrets. All girl children were given up for adoption, unbeknownst to the mother's, who were told their daughters died in childbirth or shortly thereafter. And now with the advent of modern technology, the plans were laid that the women would be sterilized after the first son was born. Theirs was the last generation that would have brothers out there in the world.

Later, Julian asked Josh if he knew anything about it.

"I knew ENKI owned several adoption agencies and boarding schools, like this one, but I never dreamed they were that determined to carry on the family line. But I can see why they do it."

"But what happens if one of the son's dies?" Julian asked.

"I don't know." Josh replied, "From what I remember in the book, it has never happened."

"That's true, there were no missed generations, were there?"

"That's pretty wild, all things considered." Josh said. "One of these day's I'm going to have to sit down and really study that book. Who knows who all we are related to, in some way."

"Well at least you didn't have a sister you didn't know about."

"I always wondered why we were 'only children', now I know. Some of us aren't."

"Do you think the others know?"

"I have no idea."

"Maybe we should find out?" Julian questioned.

"Let's save it for another time. I think Payton's too young to deal with it at the moment. He's overwhelmed as it is. Let's give him a few years to grow up some more."

"You're right. Probably best we keep it to ourselves, unless someone else asks us."

Chapter Nine

Maria was excited as she boarded the plane to London. She had spent the last week in New York City shopping and was now headed to Germany to take an offered summer internship at a university research lab.

She had traveled abroad with her parents many times as a child, but this would be her first trip overseas alone. She hoped to not only study and work hard at the university lab, but also be able to travel around Europe a bit on her own. She had already purchased her Euro pass, which would allow her to travel pretty much wherever she wished on the continent.

Once on the plane, she took a notepad and pen out of her purse and began jotting notes about New York City. She had promised to send in anonymous reports of her travels back to the editor of the campus newspaper at Radcliff. By using a pen name, it assured her of not only her privacy, but also it would allow the reports to be a bit racier than they might have been had she been forced to use her own name.

Nine hours later, the plane sat down at London's Heathrow Airport. She would have two full days in London before going on to Berlin. She planned to make the best of it, as she hailed a taxi to take her to a local hostel. She had chosen to leave her parent's money behind on this trip, much to their bewilderment, and only take what cash was absolutely necessary to see her to her job in Germany. There she would live off the stipend the university offered.

She had attempted several times to explain her reasoning to her adoptive parents, but knew she had fallen short of the goal. Her father especially, could not understand why she would want to live in poverty as he put it. She had reassured him that she would not be destitute, but needed the discipline to live within her means of what she could earn herself.

Her father had thrown his arms up in mock disgust. "I've worked all these years, for what?" He had said looking at her mother. "My little princess could have any thing in the world she wants, and what does she choose?"

Her mother also had tried to reassure him. "You know as well as I do, Martino, if she gets hungry, she'll call."

Maria's father was a Hispanic man of the old school, still not understanding why Maria preferred her studies to finding a husband. 'What had they sent her to all these fine schools for anyway', he had complained to his wife many times, 'other than to find a good husband with plenty of money to take care of her in the style she was accustomed to.'

Maria's mother had laughed at these outbursts. "We sent her to fine schools for the education it would give her." she would remind her husband, "if she finds a man there, then that is good. What shall be, shall be."

After many more words and assurances had been exchanged, Martino had finally given up trying to convince his daughter to do it differently.

"And Joshua," he tried on his final attempt, "what does he think of your plans?"

"I've told you, Daddy, Josh and I are just good friends. That's all."

"I see more than friendship when he looks at you." her father exclaimed.

"Well that's all it is, Daddy. It's all I want from him right now."

She knew that she had defeated all of her father's arguments then. Now she was unpacking her backpack at the youth hostel, deciding what to wear as she hit the town. Piccadilly Circus was to be her first stop.

Choosing a white silk blouse and khaki slacks, she went down the hallway to the bathroom to change.

As she wandered around the square, she people watched more than she shopped. Behind her, someone tapped her on the shoulder and she turned to see Payton Stone standing there.

"Payton, how good to see you. Are you home for the summer?" she asked.

"No, only for a week or two." the young man replied.

"This will be your last year at Ashleigh, won't it? I'm sure that makes you happy. Have you decided where you'll go to university?"

"My father has already decided it is to be Harvard or MIT. I'm just waiting to see which it is." he answered glumly.

"Tell you what, why don't you let me take you to dinner? We'll catch up."

Payton's face broke into a large grin. "That would be great. But I'll buy, it never hurts to spend my old man's money."

"Payton, that's downright terrible, but if you insist, who am I to argue?" she said laughing.

***

The last year had been hard on Payton. He was the last, the other twelve had all graduated and he alone had the oversized dorm room. Although they talked often, Payton still felt left out. The others were working part-time for the various companies owned by ENKI and attending Ivy League colleges in the States. He imagined them all partying and having a good time, while he was stuck here.

Several of his classmates had used the last year to constantly humiliate him in front of everyone else. One

39

boy in particular seemed to have it out for him. Daily, he would trip Payton in the hallways, catch his phone calls, especially from girls and totally embarrass him, fucking up his chances with any of them.

Payton sat on his bed, staring at the doorway. Several empty beer bottles lay on the floor beside him, half-full bottle in his hand. Lifting the bottle, he took another swig.

"Fucking asswipe." he said aloud, although there was no one in the room to hear him.

That was what had started the whole mess with Ned Grimes. He had this empty dorm room to himself. What Ned didn't understand was that he had made the request many times to the headmaster to allow roommates and the request had always been denied. Yet that didn't matter to Ned.

Payton crossed his legs and put the bottle between his legs. From his belt loop, he pulled a dagger from a hidden sheath. The dagger had been his prize the day he had been initiated into the thirteen. The gemstones imbedded into the soapstone handle gleamed in the subdued lighting of the room. Each of the thirteen had their own dagger, all made from different materials. Where Payton's was soapstone, Josh's was pure gold and Julian's pure silver. The other's made of different metals including copper, brass and nickel.

As Payton turned the blade over and over in his hand, he again wondered why his was of a material as lowly as stone. His father had attempted to explain it to him and although the explanation of "because you are the rock" sounded good, it still did not seem fair to him.

Payton felt he would always on the low end of the group. It was bad enough that he was much younger than the rest, but to be left alone here to be taunted almost constantly was just too much. Payton didn't feel it was his fault that he had not been athletic like the rest, nor was he ever interesting in putting the effort in for top grades. To his way of thinking, that was what money was for--to buy yourself into where ever you wanted to go. After his first trip to ENKI Headquarters, he never concerned himself with money thoughts. Learning what he did, had assured him that he would never want or need anything in this life.

Taking another swig of beer, draining the bottle, Payton laid the dagger on the bed. Rising, he walked to the small refrigerator in the corner and pulled out another bottle. Outside the doorway, he could hear Ned and several of the other boys talking. He couldn't make out all the words, but he did hear his own name a couple of times. Reaching for the door, he swung it open.

"What the fuck are you saying about me now, Ned?" the alcohol had given him more courage than normal.

"Just taking about what a pussy you are." the other boy responded.

Payton threw the bottle toward Ned.

"Oh, tough guy today, are we?" Ned said sarcastically.

Payton turned and slammed the door behind him. He could hear their laughter as Ned made some new comment.

"One of these days, asswipe, one of these days." Payton said as he walked over a grabbed another beer.

Returning to the bed, he reached for the dagger. Closing his eyes, he imagined cutting Ned's throat from one end to the other. He smiled as he ran his hand over the dagger blade. A dead Ned that would make him happy. Just to have him out of the way.

Payton took the dagger and ran it up his arm. The downy hairs covering the skin sliced as the blade passed by his flesh.

"It's sharp enough." he thought to himself.

For more than an hour, he sat turning the dagger over and over in his hands, stopping only to grab another beer when his bottle became empty. When the beer was gone, he switched to imported whiskey, good Irish whiskey purchased by Julian's father and given by the case as gifts to the boys. The school had no rules about drinking as long as the drinker stayed in control and did not attempt to drive. Either infraction would cause immediate expulsion.

Several shots of the smooth whiskey later, Payton rose from the bed and cracked the door of his room. The hallway was silent. He stepped out and began walking, using the walls to steady himself. Reaching Ned's door, he gently pressed his ear against the wood. All he could hear on the other side was snoring.

Quietly, he opened the door. Ned's bed was the first in the room and he quickly made his way to it. Ned was sleeping peacefully on his back, which Payton took as an omen. Leaning over, he whispered,

"No more, asswipe." as he took the dagger and ran it across the boy's throat. Pulling it away, he saw blood begin to pump from the wound.

Ned's eyes popped open. Payton grabbed the pillow from under his head and put it over his face. The terror in the other boys eyes, registered in his brain, causing him to smile in the dim light from the open hallway door.

Ned thrashed in the bed for only a few moments before he was still. Payton pulled the blood soaked pillow away from his face. The eyes, still full of terror, stared back at him. Panicking, Payton dropped the pillow on the still body and began backing away until finally, he turned and fled back through the open doorway to the safety of his own room. Shutting the door behind him, he slid to the floor.

The full knowledge of what he had done, hit him like a tree struck by lightning, forcing him to sober up. Tears ran down his cheeks, he knew that it was only a matter of time before he was questioned. He knew also, that he had never been able to lie well under pressure and that he would be a disgrace to the entirety of the thirteen.

Sobbing like he had the first day of school here, his mind kept asking, "What am I going to do?" The thought of running never crossed his mind. Suddenly he smiled.

"That's it." he said to himself. He stood and ran for the bedside table where he found his cell phone. Dialing the number, he waited. Within seconds, he was explaining to Julian just what he had done.

"Let me get a hold of Josh and we'll be on our way." Julian said calmly. "Just stay in your room till the rest of us get there."

"But, Julian...they're going to know...," his voice trailed away.

"Just stay in your room, little brother. Wash the dagger well and hide it. We'll be there as quick as we can. Before morning for sure. Got it?"

"Stay in my room... got it."

The other end of the phone went silent. Payton again sat down on the bed. Where he had been totally drunk before, clarity filled his brain now. Taking the dagger over to the small kitchenette sink, he threw it into the basin covering it with dish soap and water. Looking down at his clothes, he saw no blood on them, but his hands were covered with the red goop. Washing his hands under the running water, he took the dishrag, wiped down the phone, and then quietly did the same to the doorknob on both sides of the door. He looked down at the floor and saw just a faint print on the parquet floor, which he quickly wiped up with the rag.

Going back to the sink, he carefully scrubbed the knife to remove all traces of blood. Drying it, he placed it back into its sheath on his belt.

"Julian said hide it," he said aloud. "but where?"

Unfastening his belt, he slid the sheath from the leather as he looked frantically around the room for a place to put it. The answer came to him gradually. Years before, the boys had lifted one of the marble tiles in the bathroom and dug out a hole beneath it. He could hide the dagger there. Smiling to himself, he walked toward the bathroom. Securing the small blade under the tile, he went back to his bed to wait for Julian and the others.

As he waited, he began to smile. They would help him cover this up. They had too. That was part of being a member of the thirteen. He would get away with it and Ned would never taunt him again. Knowing that he would indeed get away with his crime, he laughed wondering to himself if he would ever experience such a wonderful emotional high again.

Chapter Ten

Within hours, Josh and Julian walked through the door.

"Now, what we're going to do is this. We have already disposed of the body." Julian said in hushed whispers. "Get your pajama's on. This is your story."

"You haven't seen Ned since last evening." Josh interrupted. "Tell the truth, the last time you saw him was when he was teasing you in the hallway."

"Yes, but...won't that make me look suspicious?"

"Normally yes, but not now. I have a girl who is going to swear she was with him last night after curfew." Julian said.

"But won't that get her into trouble?"

"Little brother, you worry too much." Julian said. "Josh will swear he was with the girl later and that he saw Ned get into his little sports car and drive off pissed."

"You really think it will work?" Payton asked.

"It will work. You just tell the truth up to the point you came back in your room. The rest of it will take care of itself."

Payton exhaled an audible sigh of relief. "You guys are the greatest. I don't know what came over me." he said. "I can't believe I did that." He hoped his face didn't show the real pleasure he felt.

"It's old history, now, Payton." Josh said. "Put it behind you, in two months you'll be out of here and the mystery of what happened to Ned will be forgotten."

"Now go to bed." Julian said. "We're out of here. Remember stick to the truth, it's easier that way."

Payton watched as the two men went out the door. The next morning, Ned was reported missing by his dorm mates. Although Payton was questioned not only by the Headmaster but also later the police, he stuck to his story.

Several weeks later, a small article appeared in the local paper asking for clues about the missing teenager. It was assumed, since his car was never found, that he had run off with an older woman and the local authorities were hoping that someone would furnish leads to calm his grieving parents.

For Payton, the last two months of school went smoothly. Without Ned to egg them on, no one else bothered him and every night before bed, he would relive the feeling of slitting Ned's throat. He always went to sleep with a smile.

***

Between classes and lab work, Maria found to her dismay she had little time for travel. A weekend jaunt here and there was about the best she could manage. Yet she had met several new people and one that was slowly becoming very special.

Anton Woods, like her, came from an upper middle class family and had worked hard to be chosen for the internship at the university. They had hit it off almost immediately. She had never met anyone from the southern part of the United States before, and his accent had been the first thing to intrigue her. Unlike her, and more like Payton, he had no problem spending the ample check that his parents sent monthly.

Together they had studied and worked together long into the summer nights. When they would finally wrap up for the evening, more often than not they would go to a beer garden and dine on German food and drink beer.

Anton had helped immensely with the articles she was sending back to the editor at Radcliff. Together they decided on the name Selma Jordon. Anton insisting that Selma was a good old-fashioned redneck name of the south. He had even opened a bank account in Selma's name and purchased a subscription service for email, so she could directly email the articles back to the college.

Asking him if he didn't think that was a bit obsessive, he had only replied that since he was planning to stay on in Germany when his internship ended, she would have the email to stay in contact with him.

She wondered if all Southerner's were as eccentric as Anton and finally decided it didn't matter, she was having fun.

The weeks passed quickly and all too soon it was time for her to return to the United States. A tearful good-bye was said at the airport as they waited for her plane. Each promised the other they would always stay in touch and Maria promised she would show him Los Angeles when he returned to the States.

For several weeks after her return to Radcliff, email flew between the two. Then suddenly they stopped, Maria sent more than twenty before she finally picked up the phone and called the lab. When she was told that Anton had died in a recent car wreck, her heart broke. Although she was once again seeing Josh, she had hoped that when Anton returned to the States something more would happen between them.

Josh had held her as she cried about her friend. He had brought flowers, candy and other gifts in an attempt to cheer her up. As the weeks passed, she finally began to feel like her old self and threw herself into her studies. Already she had received job offers, but refused to drop out of school to take any. She would not disappoint her parent's by denying them the chance to see her graduate from college with her degree.

Chapter Eleven

College graduation now behind them, the thirteen young men each took their places in the companies their fathers owned. The thirteen companies that made up ENKI were diverse, each playing a part in the behind the scenes events of the world. The Christianson Foundation, the flagship company of ENKI, specialized in feeding the world. Through research and development, they had modified numerous strains of seeds to grow in the worst drought conditions. Josh was now second in command of the foundation, answering only to his father.

Julian followed his father into the security business. Benedict Enterprises dealt not only with personal security of the thirteen, but also was responsible for heads of state and offered their services as consultants to the world's largest national security agencies, including the CIA and the now defunct KGB.

Payton was given no choice but to follow his family into the fishing industry. Although he would have preferred to have been an artist, the skills he possessed in that field were ignored and he was pushed into the genetic engineering of larger, faster growing fish.

As they each took their places in their respective fields, they then learned the truth behind ENKI. Named for the creator god of wisdom, the Endowment for Nutrition and Knowledge International had been for a millennium behind most of the world's major events. Although known by many different names in the past, the thirteen men who ran the exclusive group had worked together in each generation to shape the world.

For the elder thirteen of this generation, it was only a few more years before their work was done. Tradition made it so that as soon as the Christianson male child reached the age of thirty, he then replaced the father as chairman of the board. During a lavish ritual, which had been perfected through the generations, all thirteen sons would replace their fathers at the table.

For now, each son was expected to learn his own company, develop plans for the future and begin the search for acceptable wives in order to breed the next generation. By the age of thirty-three, each man was expected to have fathered a son who would replace him in due time.

Thirteen jets had flown into the private, desert airfield outside of Jerusalem. Aboard each were the thirteen sons. The fathers had flown in the day before as it was rule that father and son never traveled together. In over two thousand years, the rule had never been broken nor had the chair of descendency. As Josh was now twenty-eight, it was time for the new generation to learn the rest of the father's secrets. Although much of the truth had been revealed to them upon their thirteenth birthday, the total truth of what ENKI had planned for this generation had not been disclosed.

Limousines waited in a line at the end of the runway. As each son disembarked, he entered his own company vehicle where food and other refreshments were waiting. When all planes had landed and each limo filled, the caravan began the short journey to ENKI Headquarters.

As Payton stepped out of the vehicle in front of the temple like building, he was still as impressed with the structure as he had been at thirteen. Together as a group, the thirteen young men began the walk across the courtyard. As they approached the stairs, the massive doors opened and they walked inside.

"Your fathers are waiting for you in the boardroom." Old Carlisle said as he took their coats. Once his service at Ashleigh Preparatory School had been accomplished, he had been rewarded with the position of

49

Head Butler here at the headquarters. Having served the Christianson family and ENKI for years, he knew most of the secrets the building held.

"Carlisle, you're looking good." Josh said with a smile.

"Thank you sir. It is a pleasure to see all of you again." the older man replied.

Handing the coats off to other servants, Carlisle began leading the way up the marble staircase to the boardroom. Outside the double doors, each young man paused momentarily remembering the last time they had entered this room, years before.

"Any idea of what's going on?" Payton asked, looking at Carlisle.

"I'm sure you will find out in due time, young sir."

Payton's lips went into a pout. "I still don't understand all the secrecy. It's not like we're outsiders."

"Calm down, little brother." Julian said putting his hand on the younger mans shoulder. "Like Carlisle says, we'll know soon enough."

Pushing the double doors open, the young men went inside. At the table had been added thirteen extra chairs, spaced between the one's their father's occupied. Joseph Christianson rose,

"Welcome back to ENKI, sons. Please take your places."

No further instructions were needed as each young man knew to sit next to their own father. Taking their seats, they all looked toward the elder Christianson.

"Today begins a new day for you gentlemen. Today you will discover what your father's and ENKI have devoted their lives too. Today you will learn just how you can shape the coming new world."

The remaining twelve elders applauded.

"Joshua, as you know, in less than two years you will take my place at this table. The rest of you

50

gentlemen, as equally important, will support him and the goals of ENKI."

From around the table, the elders added their "hear, hears".

"We'll begin by hearing the reports of each individual company. How they have advanced toward the goal and what the future holds for each. In this way, each of you young men will know, now, what is expected of you in the future. Patrick, would you begin?"

Patrick Benedict nodded toward the elder Christianson. Walking to the end of the room, he pulled down a projector screen and dimmed the lights. Returning to the other end of the room, he snapped the switch on the waiting projector and began,

"Gentlemen, in this world we have massive poverty and starvation. While Benedict Enterprises has done all that it can behind the scenes to help alleviate this problem, we still believe that the best way is with our support of governments that choose to eradicate the problem militarily."

The screen in front of the group showed first the starving bellies of men, women and children of an unknown country. Most appeared to weak to move. As the camera panned, uniformed men carrying American machine guns entered the view. Expressionless, they began shooting the unfortunates that were unable to scramble away. Those that tried, were tracked down by others and shot in the back.

"Gentlemen, as horrible as genocide is, it is and always has been a way to keep the desperate from draining an already resource drained economy. As is happening now in Africa, it has happened the world over since the dawn of time. Benedict Enterprises will continue to help those nations that need training and armaments so that they may ensure that only the strongest survive."

Patrick Benedict flipped the projector to off. Julian had already walked to the wall and turned the lighting back up to normal.

"Gentlemen, you will receive full written reports of where we are working. Our plans in Iraq are going well. We estimate that by the end of the year, several thousand, maybe more, Iraqi undesirables will be eliminated. In that process, many Americans will die also, but... before I hear objections... the wives and children of these soldiers are already draining our own economy, by expecting not only their spouses' salaries but also welfare and food stamps from their local and state governments. They are just as undesirable as any, the world over."

Patrick Benedict sat back down in his chair. He looked at his son, searching for any reaction that would show disapproval and saw none. He smiled. As he looked around the room, he saw only acceptance from each of the men, both older and younger. Except for the younger Payton Stone. His face was white and Patrick could tell by the way he held his shoulders that his hands were clenched beneath the table. He made a mental note to tell Julian to watch the young man. Patrick knew a weak man when he saw one.

He turned back to Joseph and realized that he saw it too.

Joseph Christianson saw the look from Patrick Benedict and knew exactly what it meant. He had spent the entire presentation watching the younger men's faces. He had seen Payton wince when the armed soldiers shot the children. Now his worry was what to do about it. To his knowledge, there had never been a weak link in the thirteen before. This was Payton's second time to show weakness. The first had been the murder of his classmate. Although all members of the thirteen were proud of the way the older ones had covered up his crime, it still left a bad taste in his mouth. Payton Stone would have to be watched and watched closely. Not only by the elders, but he would have to take Josh into his confidence, so that he and Julian could keep tabs on him and his behavior also.

He stood again and introduced Thomas Fisher. His family had overseen building projects from Buckingham Palace to the Taj Majal to the White House. More recently, his company's designs had built NATO Headquarters and the UN. It was his company that had given Benedict Enterprises the precise details of just how to bring down the two towers of the World Trade Center years before. After the buildings had collapsed and the public had been allowed time to mourn, Fisher Designs had built a new trade center in the footprint of the old. A much more secure building and one with an underground bunker if the case was ever needed that they should require a secure and safe meeting place away from ENKI.

As each elder in their turn laid out the plans for the future, Joseph and Patrick watched the faces of the younger men. Each time the result was the same, Payton, while obviously trying to hide his emotional response, still showed the body language of one who could not stomach what was being done.

Finally Joseph stood.

"I suppose it is my turn, now?" he said with a smile to the others.

He picked up a small bell from in front of the stack of paper in front of him and rang it. Old Carlisle entered the room carrying a bowl of red, ripe delicious looking apples. Carlisle placed the bowl in the center of the table and left the room, closing the doors behind him.

Joseph reached over, plucked an apple from the bowl, and brought it to his lips, yet he did not take a bite, instead lowered it back down and held it in front of his chest.

"Common mythology says the apple was the downfall of man. Fitting then, is that the Christianson

Foundation has developed an apple that because of its genetic engineering will rid the world of many of the undesirable elements that The Thirteen has been trying to eradicate for centuries."

Joseph saw the shock that filled the other men's faces. Other than Patrick, no member of the thirteen had been privileged to this information. The research and development of the apple seed had been split between many laboratories and facilities, so that no single scientist knew exactly what he was working on.

"But, how...?" Thomas' voice said quietly.

"These apples hold the ability to sterilize the next generation of those that consume them. While the original partaker of the apple, just as in Eden, will still bear fruit, it will be the offspring that are truly punished."

"You mean... mass sterilization?"

"Exactly, gentlemen. Once a man or a woman eats of this fruit, their offspring is forever rendered sterile."

"So how do we control it?" Andrew's voice sounded the question on everyone's lips.

"Through the foundation. Not only do we ship the apples into starving populations, we also plant the trees so that in time, all of the unknowing will avail themselves of the fruit."

"I still don't see the control. How will we stop others, those not undesirable, from eating these apples?" Thomas asked.

"Always doubting, are you not Thomas? The places we send these apples to will not be frequented by the deserving. Yes, we will have to have tight control, but by the same token,... we all know that it is the branding that entices the have's to buy a product. To that end, we will supply the better's stores and mail order catalogues with an even superior fruit than this. It will be no problem, trust me."

Thomas' face still looked skeptical as Joseph continued,

"By marketing the unaltered fruit to the high-end market, most will believe that what we are supplying to the world's poor and hungry is the leftovers of the crop -- i.e., an inferior product."

"Has this been done with any other fruit?" Nathan asked looking up from the notes he had been scribbling.

"No. For now, one product is more than sufficient. If we see results that are not up to expectations, then we would be willing to discuss other means."

Matthew Barrister sat back in his leather seat. He brought his hands up to chin level in almost prayer like fashion.

"That is utterly brilliant, Joseph."

Patrick Benedict laughed. "So true, if we can't fight them out, if we can't tax them out, if we can't starve them out... well, hell... we'll breed them out."

Every man in the room smiled, even Payton Stone.

Joseph rang the small bell once more and Carlisle appeared in the doorway.

"Carlisle will you dispose of the apples. Make sure no one on staff eats them."

"I'll put them down the disposal myself."

"You're a good man, Carlisle. I am glad you are back with us."

"Thank you, sir." the older man said as he took the bowl from the table and left the room.

"Gentlemen, do not forget that tomorrow night is the ENKI Charity Ball in New York." Joseph said as he looked around the room. "Young Gentlemen, it is also time for you to begin narrowing the field for your future wives. Many proper young women will be in attendance, so I'm sure you will be able to expand on your options. As for us older folk, since the competition will be fierce, I expect we'll just watch and see the younger generation at

55

work. I hear it's changed a bit since I was on the prowl and had to make the decision."

"A wife?" Payton said aloud. "I'm only twenty five."

"Never too soon to start looking, son." the elder Stone said.

Payton, like his father before him, had no desire to be married. He lived and loved the life of the playboy - a different woman every night. A wife would cramp his style. Payton knew he was good looking and all the amenities that money could buy. That attracted women like magnets and he had no thoughts of giving it up.

He would marry in his time, but it would be long after Josh had married and conceived the child that would carry on the line. He wouldn't wait as long as his own father had, he knew too well the heartbreak of being so much younger than the rest. Yet he knew Josh had no plans to marry anytime in the near future and so he put the thought from his brain.

His father had chosen his job and his profession, he was not going to allow him to choose how he would live for the next two years also. After that, Josh would be the leader and things would be much different. He would be his own man then.

Chapter Twelve

Josh arrived at the ball with Maria on his arm. As they strolled up the red carpet, the assembled paparazzi quickly snapped picture after picture. Julian followed behind, Sandy Bickford a well-known cover girl and model, holding on to his arm. After allowing the photographers to have their moment, Julian leaned forward to Josh.

"Don't you think that's enough?" he asked.

"Probably so. But it will play well in the press." Josh answered. "Besides, got to have some fun. You know it's going to be boring as hell in there." he said nodding toward the door.

"I hear that. I hate these monkey suits. I wonder if the others are here yet."

"If not, they'll be here soon. I wonder if Payton has a date."

"Speaking of Payton, I need to talk to you about him. Something my father said yesterday." Julian said in a low whisper.

"My father said something also. Lunch tomorrow?"

"That sounds good." Julian reached the glass doors of the building.

Inside the party was well underway. Each man mingled with the crowd, showing off their dates and looking for the other members of their group. Josh caught his father's eye, who nodded with approval and smiled back at him. Several hours later, he found Payton sitting at a far corner table. Barely awake, obviously having drunk too much champagne. Leaving Maria with him, Josh went to find Julian. Far better to get Payton out of here before the crowd and the father's realized the state he was in.

Making it look as if they were going to another party, they escorted Payton out of the building. Traveling in one limo, they took him back to his apartment where they put him to bed and then took the ladies home.

At the entrance to Julian's condo, Josh said,

"Definitely lunch tomorrow."

"Definitely." Julian responded.

Both men wondered if Payton was totally out of control. They knew he had a drinking problem, but had felt that they had kept it fairly well contained. Yet tonight's behavior and the conversations with their father's the day before made them both wonder exactly what to do next.

Josh was already seated at the Tavern on the Green Restaurant when Julian arrived near noon. Ordering a steak and potato with a scotch neat, Julian looked over at his lifelong friend.

"I think we have a bigger problem than we thought." he said.

"I agree." Josh said taking a sip of the dark beer he was drinking. "But the question is, what do we do?"

'I've already put a team of men on him. To watch, see what he's doing. They will keep him out of trouble." Julian said. "My father says he'll never be able to fulfill his responsibilities to ENKI... "

"That's about what mine said yesterday. This is the big problem though. They are meeting again today, without Payton's father, to discuss the future. I think they are looking at a future without us taking over."

"They have to turn it over, don't they? It's tradition."

"I think they will, but unlike the generations before, I don't think they will give up total control. That's what worries me."

"So what do we do? We've earned this... it belongs to us." Julian said emphatically.

58

"I have some ideas." Josh said. "Order yourself another drink, we've got lots of talking to do."

Once the drinks were served, Josh began filling Julian in on what he felt they would have to do. Julian said little, only asking a question here and there and nodding in agreement.

"So could you find us who we need?" Josh asked.

"Without a problem. It will take a while though. We are going to have to be very discreet. And the others, do you think they will go along?"

"We aren't going to give them a choice, but yes, once we explain the circumstances, they will do it willingly." Josh said.

"And Payton?"

"Payton will do as he is told. He, most of all, will have no choice. Not if he wants his chair at the table. And we both know how important that is to him."

"When do you want all this to take place, Josh? How much time to I have?"

"We have to keep tradition, Jules. We'll plan it for the day that we are ritually given control. My birthday, next year. Think you can manage?

"Plenty of time." Julian responded, slinging back another shot. "Plenty of time."

Chapter Thirteen

Josh and Julian sat on cushions with their backs to the wall behind the sheer curtains in the small opium den outside Hong Kong. Every now and again, a small older Chinese woman would come and fill their glass with a dark brew.

"You think he will show?" Josh asked.

"He'll show." Julian answered.

Moments later, a man of middle-eastern descent entered behind the little woman. He took a seat opposite the two men. No pleasantries exchanged as the younger men stared at the new arrival.

"The timing is critical." Josh said to the man.

"We will time it perfectly." the man replied with a thick accent.

"There can be no mistakes. Nothing can be tied back to us. Is this fully understood?" Julian asked.

"It is understood. We will set everything up but do nothing until the call is received."

Julian reached under the table and pulled out a large leather briefcase.

"As agreed, half now. The remainder when the job is completed."

The man opened the case and examined the contents. Full of hundred dollar bills, he seemed satisfied and closed the case. Standing, he bowed toward the two men.

"Gentlemen, I will await your call."

Julian nodded to the man, dismissing him and he disappeared the way he had entered.

"Everyone is with us?" Julian asked.

We all agree. Even Payton needed no real encouragement. I did not realize just how much he hated his father." Josh replied.

"But do you think they will all follow through?" Julian asked.

"If we begin, they will follow. Have no doubt." Josh answered.

The plane set down at Denver airport. Josh hated flying commercial, but the layover this trip promised was a good opportunity to meet with the others without raising suspicion. He had called for all of the younger thirteen to meet at Bart's hunting lodge in Vale. Now that his plans had been finalized, it was time to tell the others what was expected of them.

As they disembarked from the plane and went to a waiting rental car, Josh was aware that his friend was unusually quiet. Julian had said little on this leg of the journey back to Los Angeles.

"What is bothering you, Jules?'

"Just thinking." came Julian's short reply.

As they got in the car and Julian maneuvered away from the airport, he finally broached the subject of what was on his mind.

"I'm still not sure that the others will go along with this. Bart and Andrew have great relationships with their fathers. Matt too."

"They will go along with it. I'll see to that. They all stand to lose as much as we do."

"But will they see it that way?"

Josh sat back in the seat smiling. "I'll make sure they do. It's not going to be a problem, Jules. They have always listened to me."

Julian again wandered back into his own mind, remaining silent and focusing on the drive to Vale. He still had doubts, yet knew that Josh could be very persuasive when needed. As he pulled into the drive of the hunting lodge, he had convinced himself that Josh would bring the others along.

Entering the building and going straight to the great room, Josh asked,

"Anyone not here yet?"

Looking around the room, Julian saw that both Matt and Nathan had not yet arrived.

"Nate and Matt are riding together. They just called and should be here shortly." Bart answered.

Josh went to the sideboard and poured himself a drink. In the hallway, he heard the front door open and close and within moments, Matthew and Nathan had joined the rest in the room.

"Well..." Josh began, "Now that we are all here, I'll tell you why I called us together.

Three hours later, even Thomas, the one man of the group who like his father questioned everything that was proposed, all men had agreed to Josh's plan. There was no turning back now. ENKI would be theirs, and theirs alone. Josh's mood soared as he and Julian returned to the rental car to drive back to Denver to catch their flight. Even Julian seemed more jovial as he drove.

"You did it Josh. Got to hand to you."

"I knew they would go along. Hate to say 'I told you so' but..." Josh laughed.

"Really I had no doubt you would get it done, Josh. I just really thought it would take longer."

"What can I say, Jules. We are all a bunch of ruthless bastards." Josh replied, still laughing.

***

Maria was frustrated. Two things in her life bothered her. Her thirtieth birthday had come and gone and she was still no closer to discovering who her real parents were. That and the fact that she had been dating Josh almost exclusively since she was seventeen and that appeared to be going nowhere fast either.

62

Her adoptive parents had died several years earlier and although they had attempted to help her with her search, no amount of research could disclose the names of her birth parents. The adoption agency swore the records of her birth and adoption had been destroyed in a flood shortly after her adoption had been finalized. She could not find any court records either, those too had been lost supposedly in the same flood. Full of doubts, she had checked with the local newspapers and found that indeed there had been a massive flood in the year after her birth, totally destroying paper documents in both the courthouse and several offices located nearby.

Josh too, remained an enigma to her. When they were together, life was good. Yet she still heard rumors of his seeing other women. If the rumors were true, they were usually lower class women who were willing to do some of the kinkier things that Josh seemed to like in the bedroom. Yet when she would confront him, he inevitably put her fears to rest, telling her it was only the media and those jealous of him and his position.

Some days she didn't know what to believe. The only thing she was sure of was her love for him. She had fallen hard at the first school dance they attended together and had never really looked at another man since. Even her summer romance with Anton in Germany never competed with her feelings for Josh. Thinking they would marry after college, she first slept with him one summer's night during her sophomore year. Now, almost ten years later, marriage had still not been mentioned between them. Yet, she couldn't say that she was totally dissatisfied. Josh was a skilled and wonderful lover and the times they had together were always memorable. With him, she had seen the world.

She now had a job with Crytech Research, a firm owned by Andrew's Cryton's family. Maria did not know how much pull Josh had used with his old friend and roommate to get the job with Crytech and really didn't care. It paid well and allowed her to pursue her passion.

Convinced as a small child by imagination alone that her parents had given her up because they could not afford to feed a child, she became obsessed with finding an answer to the hunger problem the world over. After years of hard study, she was now in a position at Crytech to become one of the leaders in developing a low cost food source for the world's most desperate regions.

Crytech Research had been long working on the same problem and when they offered her the job after she obtained her Master's Degree, she could hardly hide her enthusiasm. She felt she was only a few years away from a major breakthrough. Then and only then, would she truly worry about marriage. Until then, her part time relationship with Josh was more than enough as she didn't want her energy divided between work and marriage. There would be time for husband and children later.

Maria looked up at the clock on the mantle. Enough rambling, she thought to herself. It was time to get ready for her date with Josh. Having no idea where they were going, she decided to dress classy casual, pulled a pair of ivory colored silk slacks from the closet, and paired that with a light blue silk shirt, using a wide black leather belt to tie it together. Slipping her feet into black leather loafers, she tied a black silk scarf around her long auburn hair. Looking at herself in the mirror, she knew she looked good. Taking a jacket that matched the pants from the closet, she walked to the living room and laid it across a wing-backed chair.

Money had never been a problem for her, and although she was thrifty by nature, she knew she would never want for anything. Her adoptive parents had left her a trust fund that would not only take care of her for a lifetime, but several generations after her if needed.

While waiting for Josh to arrive, she opened her laptop to check for recent email. Only one new message was waiting and like most she received, it was a request for money. Years earlier, she had made the mistake of giving a healthy donation to what turned out to be an unscrupulous charity and now several others hounded her looking for a handout also. She deleted the email at the same time she heard the knock on the door. Closing the laptop down, she went to greet Josh.

Opening the door, she was surprised to see not only Josh, but Julian standing there also.

"Hope you don't mind, but we've got a third wheel this evening." Josh said, his face suppressing laughter.

Maria didn't mind at all. Julian had become a close friend over the years and often accompanied them on trips and other excursions. Back when they were teens, she had once considered the dark skinned man a serious suitor, but for some reason unknown to her, that came to a halt when he stated, "I really just want to be friends."

Although it had confused her at the time, she was now happy that she had a friend as wonderful as he had turned out to be.

"And so, where are you wonderful gentlemen taking me this evening?" she asked.

"There's a new club that just opened in West Hollywood." Julian said. "We thought it would be cool to go check it out."

"Am I dressed okay?" she asked.

"You look... perfect." Josh said, putting his arm around her shoulders. "You ready."

"Always." she said, returning his smile.

Locking the apartment behind her, the three quickly made their way to the waiting limo. Once inside, Josh said,

"I wanted to make tonight a bit special. It may be a week or two before you see me again."

"Another business trip?" she asked.

"Isn't it always?" he replied.

"So where you off to this time?"

"Hong Kong." Julian answered, saying the words in a mock oriental fashion.

Maria smiled. "How long will you be gone?"

"I'm not sure yet. At least a week, maybe longer." Josh said.

"I'll miss you." she said, "I'll miss both of you."

"Well if we can work it out and you can tear yourself away from the lab, maybe I'll send the jet back for you in a couple of days."

"I would love to see Hong Kong again, but I am really swamped at work. So much new data coming in." She smiled at Josh, watching his reaction. "Maybe you can live without me for a week or two."

"I probably can." he replied laughing, "but who will Julian have to pick on?"

"I'm sure he can manage to just pick on you."

Chapter Fourteen

The boardroom was somber as the thirteen young men together entered through the doors. All pictures had been taken from the walls, the chandelier removed from the ceiling. All that remained was the round table, the chairs and the book of lineage. Candles were lit, sitting on the floor around the perimeter of the room. A large gold menorah, with all candles lit, stood in the middle of the mahogany table.

The father's stood at their places awaiting the signal from Joseph to begin. The older men wore ritual robes in various, but different jewel tone colors. Joseph pulled his ceremonial dagger from the sheath attached to the tie around his waist. Bringing it to his lips, he kissed the blade and laid it upon the teak inlay of the table in front of him. Each man around the table repeated the procedure.

Andrew, the first to be called was surprised to see Carlisle appear from out of nowhere. Helping him remove his jacket, the old man instructed Andrew to strip. Upon doing so, Old Carlisle handed him a robe in the same gemstone color as his father.

"Andrew Cryton, approach the table and face your father." Joseph's voice beckoned.

Andrew approached the table, slowly and solemnly.

The elder Cryton lifted the dagger and held it to his son's throat. Andrew's eyes widened, but he said nothing.

"Andrew Cryton, do you swear your allegiance to your lord and master Jesus Christ?"

"I do."

"Will you do all in your power to serve and protect his progeny, work in unison with the others to further the goals of this generation of the thirteen?"

"I will."

"Will you give oath to never reveal this organization, nor its past, present or future existence to anyone other than your first born son?"

"I do."

"Andrew Cryton, do you pledge that within the next three years you will have fathered a son to replace you when the time has come, in order to fulfill your obligations to the tradition and guaranteed survival of the thirteen."

"I swear."

The elder Cryton once more kissed the blade of the dagger. He handed it to his son, who in turn did the same.

"Andrew Cryton, You will now take your father's place at the table. You are now fully one of the thirteen."

Taking the dagger and replacing it on the table, Andrew watched as his father stepped away from the table and stood against the wall.

With what appeared to be no particular order, each son was called to the table to face his father, the ritual was repeated, until only Josh, Julian, and Payton remained. When Payton's name was called next, he eagerly stepped forward. Once in his robe, he was called to the table.

As the tip of the dagger touched his throat, he winced involuntarily and took a deep breath. He listened to the words being spoken and answered all in the affirmative. An added question was laid before him.

"Payton Stone, you are the rock of this foundation, do you pledge that you recognize Joshua Christianson as the incarnate of Jesus Christ? That you will never deny or betray neither him nor any other member of the thirteen?"

Payton's face registered shock as he heard the lines. After a long silence, he finally uttered, "I do."

As his father handed him the dagger, a small smile crept into the corners of his lips.

Julian was called next. His ritual too, had an extra pledge.

"Julian Benedict, do you swear that you would give your life in protecting each member of the thirteen. Will you apply extra diligence to the safekeeping of your lord and master and the next generation he shall begin?"

Without hesitation, Julian answered, "I will."

Moments later, Josh's name was called. As he stripped down, he was presented a robe that even in the dim light of the room was brilliant in its whiteness. Stepping forward to the table, his fathers platinum dagger was raised to his throat.

"Joshua Christianson, do you accept that you are the incarnate of Jesus Christ, the son of God?"

"I do."

"Do you accept the responsibilities of this incarnation? Will you lead your disciples, as your forefather did, to create a world that is better than the one before you?"

"I will."

"Do you swear that you will continue on the descendency line, that you will have a son before the age of thirty-three, that you will bring this group back together on that child's thirtieth birthday to continue the next generation of the thirteen?"

"I will."

As Josh's ritual came to a close, each elder returned to the table. Once again, Old Carlisle appeared pushing a tray that held twenty-six gold goblets, each studded at the base with thirteen jewels. Filling the chalices with a deep red wine, he handed one to each man in the room. When every man held a goblet in his hand, the elderly man pushing the now empty trolley left the room.

Joseph Christianson raised his glass, "To the next generation -- the thirteen men who rule the world."

As the elders tipped their goblets in unison, the younger men stepped behind them.

"To our fathers who have given us life... May they rest in peace." Josh said as he ran the edge of his own dagger across his father's throat. His father fell in a heap into the stuffed leather chair. Before anyone could react, every son had followed Josh's lead.

As the elder thirteen sat quickly dying in their chairs, Josh reached for his goblet. Raising it in a new toast, he said,

"What is done, is done. As we now go our separate ways for a while, may we always remember the oaths we took here today. The thirteen shall live forever."

Each took a drink from the goblet and smiled.

Moments later, Old Carlisle entered the room. Upon seeing what had happened, he let out a small scream. Josh quickly walked up to him, while Julian went behind.

"Carlisle, you have been a faithful servant. Your years of devotion to our fathers and to us will never be forgotten." Josh smiled, and the old man seemed to relax a bit.

From behind him, the gleam of Julian's blade sparkled in the candlelight. With a quick motion, he ran it across the old man's throat. Josh stepped out of the way as the man fell to the floor.

"Gentlemen, I believe it is time to take our leave. Be sure to forget nothing."

Around the table, the new generation began by removing the dagger sheaths from the ties on their father's robes and replacing the larger daggers from the table. Wiping the blood on their father's robes, they replaced their own original smaller daggers to their sheaths. They then collected the chalices by dumping the remaining contents to the floor.

Josh walked over to the small podium and picked up the Book of Descendency.

"Too bad about the table, I always thought it was a beautiful piece of furniture." Julian said.

"We'll have another built." Josh replied. "Shall we go?"

The thirteen men exited the boardroom, locking the door behind them. Within hours, each was in a different part of the world.

Chapter Fifteen

Josh and Julian stood nursing dark ales in the small English country pub. The television above the simple bar was finishing up programming for the day and beginning to broadcast the late edition BBC News. Only a few hours earlier, they had stopped at an out of the way phone box and placed a quick call.

With scenes of a flaming building behind him, the newscaster began his report,

"A major explosion rocked the desert outside Jerusalem just moments ago. Rushing to this site, it has been discovered that the building housing the Endowment for Nutrition and Knowledge International, ENKI for short has been bombed. Few details are available at this time, but looking at the damage from here, it appears that the ancient building has crumbled completely onto itself. So far, no organization has taken responsibility for this blast. We will keep you updated as information is released."

Simultaneously the cell phones in both Josh and Julian's pockets rang. Answering them quickly, they told the caller of their whereabouts and insisted that they would be at the site soon. The pub keeper stood directly behind them at the bar, and could see emotion fill their faces. Throwing money on the bar, they quickly left the pub.

Arriving at the private airstrip outside Jerusalem, they were greeted by the Israeli police along with security forces hired by Benedict Enterprises.

"I am afraid your fathers are dead." an Israeli captain told them as they walked toward the waiting cars.

"How did this happen?" Julian said to the security guard.

"We don't know yet." the guard said, his voice shaky.

"Find out and find out now." Julian stormed, "Find out who allowed this breach of security and send them to me."

"Yes, sir." the frightened guard said.

"How many dead?" Josh asked the captain.

"We are not sure. So far, only one servant has escaped. A maid, she told us that there were fourteen servants on duty, and that all thirteen members of ENKI were in meeting." the captain replied. "We can assume that she is the only person to make it out alive."

Josh looked stricken. "All of the ENKI board members are dead?"

"I fear so, sir."

"Call the others, get them here." Josh said to Julian. To the captain, he said, "Take us there."

They traveled quickly to the burning remains of ENKI. The entire structure was leveled.

"Was this a terrorist act?" Julian asked the captain.

"We feel it had to be. This took careful and detailed planning. No loner could have accomplished this." the captain replied.

"Can you find us a hotel?" Josh asked.

The captain started to speak, when Julian cut him off, "Already done, Josh. We have secured a small hotel in Jerusalem that will house all of us."

Josh looked at the captain, "I wish to be informed personally with any additional information you receive. No matter how minute or how insignificant you may believe it to be. Now if you will, take us to the hotel where we can await the others."

Later, inside a large conference room at the hotel, the thirteen gathered.

"There weren't supposed to be any survivors." Payton said, rage on his face.

"It was just a maid, a kitchen one at that." Josh said dismissingly.

"But she might know we were there." Payton said.

"She might, but I doubt it. One thing I will give our father's credit for... " Julian began, "is hiring tight lipped servants. They never talked among themselves except for duties."

"I hope to hell you're right." Payton said, his voice still filled with anger.

"Don't worry, Payton. Our kindness to her now, will more than keep any secrets she knows quiet." Andrew said.

"What kindness?" Payton asked.

"Right now, our representatives are offering her and her entire family refuge in the United States. Away from this war zone. She will accept, rest assured." Nathan said quietly.

"And the police here will let her leave?" Payton questioned.

"Of course they will. We own them." Josh said, smiling as he shook his head. Usually it was Thomas so full of doubt.

Josh stood up and turned on the television set. Changing channels, he found an English news channel.

As the broadcast began, a note was passed to the anchor.

"This just in," he began, "a Muslim terrorist group, Jundallah has just claimed responsibility for today's bombing of ENKI headquarters here in Jerusalem. Their letter reads in part, "The one world capitalist that have plagued Moslems and the world for generations have been sent to meet their gods. May Allah be praised and may his servants find their place in heaven. End of quote.

As most world watcher's know about Jundallah is that it is a terrorist group that has its roots in the uprising of Al-Qaeda in the early parts of this millennium. They have continually grown bolder in their assaults upon a peaceful world."

The journalist looked down at his notes, "We will now join Roger Crater of the BBC for his reaction to this news."

Josh flipped off the television. "See Payton, I told you. No problems. The entire world will now be trying to find these guys."

Payton didn't answer, just sat staring at Josh.

"Don't you get it Payton, little brother? This is the biggest thing to happen in the world since September 11, 2001."

"What happened then?" Payton asked.

"Did you skip your history classes?" Thomas asked, laughing.

"Nine Eleven is when the old World Trade Center in New York City was taken out by Muslim hijackers. Thousands were killed, many more injured." Josh said, offhandedly.

"The same Muslim group that this attack is being linked to." Thomas said.

"I still don't get the significance." Payton said, his voice pouty.

"The significance is -- the last time it plunged the world into war. Country against country. This time, every country will unite together -- ENKI represents all countries. We will gain even more control over national leaders, they will be our voice at the UN." Josh replied.

"Enough history lesson for today." Julian interrupted, "We should begin planning our father's memorials."

"We should." Andrew agreed.

"And once that is done, like a phoenix, ENKI will rise again out of the ashes." Josh said.

Every man in the room smiled.

Chapter Sixteen

Less than a year later, the thirteen stood in front of the large red ribbon surrounding the new ENKI Headquarters. Built on the same land as the old, the new building was modern, with clean lines and abundant glass. Each man stood with one hand on the ribbon, the other hand holding on oversized pair of scissors.

Josh spoke for the group, while hundreds of approved dignitaries, including heads of state looked on. Repeating the lines that he had said in the hotel months earlier,

"As the phoenix rises from the ashes, so has The Endowment for Nutrition and Knowledge International. ENKI is and always has been inspired by the heavens and no man, or groups of men will ever be able to destroy it."

At that point, each man cut the ribbon. "Ladies and Gentlemen, please join us inside for cocktails and conversation." Josh finished. The oversized glass doors swung open and he led the way inside.

The air-conditioned reception hall was a welcome refuge from the arid desert heat outside. As Josh and the others mingled with the guests, they listened carefully to the conversations around them. Although tiny cameras and microphones hidden throughout the room were recording every gesture and word spoken, each man watched the eyes and body language of the guests around them. The tapes would be reviewed later.

Not only would the information retrieved from the tapes help them determine their true allies, it had been proven in the past that many times unguarded conversations gave good fodder to use against their enemies. The thirteen knew they had enemies, none that were overtly outspoken, but that worked behind the scenes in many governments trying to wrestle power away from them. Those confirmed often met with untimely deaths, either accidental or tragic whichever case suited best.

Hours later, the last guest gone, the thirteen men sat alone in the reception hall. Servants darted to keep their glasses full of the beverage of choice. Around them, champagne glasses sat and laid on tables everywhere, along with dirty plates and crumbled napkins. Several maids were already at the task of cleaning up the room.

"At least that is over with." Andrew said quietly.

"Do you think we came off all right?" Thomas asked.

"I think it went well. Everyone who was invited came... but then again, who would dare not to show. It was as much in their best interest to be here as it was ours." Julian said in answer.

Josh stood and stretched. "Shall we go upstairs. I for one need a good nights sleep."

The others nodded their assent. The third and fourth floors of the new building were lavishly outfitted apartments. The fifth floor housed the penthouse belonging to Josh. Covering the entire width and breath of the structure, every room inside was large and airy. Julian maintained a smaller apartment inside the penthouse.

Josh walked out into the entryway. The circular staircase leading upward overwhelmed the room. Looking upward, he shook his head and led the way to the elevators camouflaged in the far wall.

Inside the penthouse, Julian looked at Josh. "Did you notice Payton's up to old tricks again?"

Josh nodded. Coming up in the elevator, Payton was almost incoherently drunk. Josh didn't care what he did on his own time, but when he was here or any other ENKI function he was going to have to stay sober.

"Should I talk to him?" Julian asked.

"No." Josh shook his head. "We'll confront him with it tomorrow. Hold him accountable. Let him know that this will not be tolerated."

"Think that will be enough?" Julian asked.

Josh shrugged. "Probably not. Who's that girl he's been seeing? Amelia... ?"

"Amelia Cardovy. Nice girl."

"Think she'd make a good wife?"

"Good family, good breeding." Julian answered.

"Then let's marry him off. Maybe she can help keep him in line."

"I doubt that, but it's worth a try."

***

Payton sat on the overstuffed sofa of his fourth floor apartment with a drink in his hand. On the lacquered table in front of him stood an opened bottle of scotch. His mind, drunk with not only alcohol but also anger raged inside of him. 'Who was he to decide that it was time for bed?' his mind questioned as he thought of Josh. 'Am I still a little boy who needs Old Carlisle to tell me it's time to turn out the lights?'

Payton's anger at Josh had been growing steadily for the last year. More so since the bombing of ENKI. Every idea Payton had, Josh squashed without ever listening to any argument he had. All his life, he had been forced to follow Josh's lead. All his life, he had had to listen to Josh as a leader. His leader. He never asked for that. Even when he swore allegiance to Josh at the ritual, he had felt it unfair. Why was Josh the chosen leader. Why not him? He was just as qualified. His ancestor had done just as much, if not more, to further the causes of the thirteen.

Payton threw back another shot of scotch. All night long, he had listened to other people sing the praises

79

of ENKI. Each and every time Josh got the credit. Never once did he hear his name mentioned. Always Josh.

Then there was Julian. Always watching him. Always criticizing. And Josh always listening. Payton had suspicions that Julian was having him followed, but as yet been unable to catch anyone in the act. Julian could do no wrong in Josh's eyes. Hell, he could do no wrong in any of the others eyes. It was always Payton that they questioned.

Payton leaned back on the sofa. Tomorrow was the vote. Tomorrow it would be decided if they would carry on their father's original plan or carry it further. He knew he just as well vote with the others, because whatever Josh proposed would be followed by the rest. And he knew, no matter what, he would have no part in it.

Payton wished that Amelia were here. He could use a good piece of ass right now. But no, Josh had decreed that no woman was to ever enter the living quarters here. He knew also, that if he tried to leave, to go into the city, someone would stop him.

He closed his eyes and the room seemed to be spinning. "I hate him." was his last thought before passing out.

Payton awoke to the pounding on the door of the apartment. Stumbling to the door, he swung it open to find Julian standing there.

"The meeting began thirty minutes ago. We are waiting for you." the anger in Julian's face startled him. "You have ten minutes to make yourself presentable and get downstairs."

"I'm not a child." Payton stammered.

"As you act, so shall you be treated." Julian responded before he turned and walked away.

Payton slammed the door to Julian's retreating form. The bang hurt his head. Still feeling the effects of the alcohol from last night, he muttered to himself, "I'll show up when I damn well please."

Yet he still went into the bathroom, stripped and took a shower. The heat of the water only intensified his headache. Opening the medicine cabinet, he pulled out a prescription bottle of pain pills. Popping two into his mouth, he washed them down with water from the bathroom sink.

Still muttering intelligibly to himself, he walked into the master bedroom to the large walk in closet. Pulling a shirt from the rack, he slid it on his still damp body. Grabbing suit pants from another hanger, he yanked them up his legs, not bothering to put on underwear. He pulled a tie from the rack and slid it around his neck.

His head still banging, he walked with the suit jacket to the bed where he slid on his socks and shoes. Putting his jacket on as he went out the door, he walked to the elevator. Nine minutes after Julian's ultimatum, he entered the boardroom where everyone was sipping coffee, waiting for him.

Smiling he said as he made his way to his place at the table. "Sorry I'm late, I overslept."

Josh smiled back at him. "No Payton, not overslept, over indulged."

Payton looked around at the faces in the room. They all looked at him coldly.

"I don't see what the problem is. So I got a little drunk last night." Payton responded, immediately going on the defensive.

"No, Payton, you did not get a 'little' drunk last night, you got a lot drunk. You did this in front of others. You embarrassed not only yourself, but you also were a dirty spot on the thirteen as a whole."

"You're making too much of this... " Payton began.

"I haven't even begun." Josh cut him off. "Either you get your drinking under control, to our satisfaction, or... "

"Or what?" Payton voice dripped with sarcasm, "You'll ban me from the thirteen?"

Josh once again at Payton, his blue eyes looking like cold steel. "No Payton, we will not ban you from the thirteen. We will eliminate you."

"You can't do that." Payton stammered. "The thirteen works as a whole. It always has."

Josh sat down and leaned back in his chair.

"Have you ever read the Christian Bible, Payton?"

Payton, still unbelieving at what was being said, slowly shook his head no.

"In the Christian Bible, the story is told of one disciple who betrayed Christ. One story ends with that disciple being murdered, the other with him killing himself."

"But..."

"According to Christian Tradition," Josh continued, "Only eleven disciples carried on."

"But mine was your rock..."

"Yes, my rock. Yet he denied me three times, according to tradition. That is why those lines were in your swearing in. You have already denied me, Payton. Will you be the one that betrays me also."

Payton suddenly felt like his legs would not support him. As the others stared at him, he responded,

"I'll do whatever you want." Payton knew he was defeated. If he didn't follow, he knew from Josh's thinly veiled threat, he would be killed.

"That you will have to prove." Josh said.

"How?" Payton asked, his voice flat, all defiance gone.

"We talked as we waited for you. We all agree you need some stability in your life. Marry Amelia."

"I'm not ready to get married..." Payton began to protest, but his voice trailed off.

"When we leave here today, you will go to London and propose to Amelia. We all expect wedding invitations in six months or less."

"And if she refuses me?"

"Then you will find someone that will. Or we will find her for you."

Payton opened his mouth, once more to protest then saw the look in Julian's eyes and said, "All right. Whatever everyone thinks is best."

Josh stood again, "Now that that bit of unpleasantness is out of the way, shall we get down to business?"

Each man in the room nodded his affirmative.

***

As scheduled, Payton's wedding to Amelia Cardovy took place within the allotted six-month timeframe. A lavish affair, costing the brides family thousands of pounds, Josh stood as Payton's best man.

At the reception, each of the thirteen offered their congratulations to the couple and danced with the bride. Amelia appeared happy and radiant, Payton somber.

"Cheer up, little brother." Julian said as he pulled Payton aside, away from the guests. "Marriage can't be that bad."

"How would you know?" the younger man asked.

"I don't. But I am thinking of doing it myself. Eventually." Julian smiled.

"Well at least YOU won't be told who and when to marry."

"I don't know about that, little brother."

"I wish you would quit calling me that." Payton said. "I've hated that all my life."

"Should have said something sooner. It's a habit now."

"So break the habit." Payton responded.

"Easier said than done, little brother." Julian laughed as he walked away, leaving Payton alone in the garden.

"Damn him." Payton whispered under his breath. "I need a drink."

He began walking toward the open bar at the end of the garden. Before he reached it, a waiter approached carrying champagne on a tray. Payton reached for a glass and downed it quickly. The waiter stood silently as he replaced the empty glass on the tray and picked up another. "I'll put this one on the bar." Payton told the waiter as he started once again for the open bar where the 'real' liquor was being served.

At the bar, Payton drained the champagne from the goblet in his hand and sat it down. "Scotch neat." he told the approaching bartender.

Payton turned and surveyed the crowd. He could see none of the other thirteen and hoped they were all in the hall dancing. He knew he, himself, would have to get back there soon. Yet rationalized that there was enough time for another drink or two.

Four shots later, he entered the hall to find his new bride.

***

Maria was having a wonderful time at the wedding. It was hard to believe that Payton was the first of the group to get married as he had always seemed to be the most immature one to her. As Josh introduced her to the girl friends and dates of the others, she guessed several of them would soon be following Payton's lead.

84

She didn't get that impression from Josh. He still seemed in no hurry to marry. But today, she wasn't going to worry about that. She had other things on her mind. Things that didn't make sense. Raw data that she would shove to the back of her mind and try to dismiss as impossible. Then she would see Andrew, be reminded of work and it would all come flooding back to the forefront once more.

One of her research students at Crytech had brought her data she had requested on fruit seeds. In her efforts to genetically attempt to strengthen food sources to better survive harsh environments, she had branched out from the wheat, corn and soybeans that for years had held promise but no major breakthroughs.

Yet, the data from the fruit confused her. One strain of apple seed appeared to be totally sterile. Unable to reproduce itself and she didn't understand why. They had tried for months to germinate the seed and to date still failed. And no one could trace the source of the seed either.

The records of purchase could not be found, nor did any of her students admit to bringing in unverified outside specimens. The whole situation confused and confounded her. None of it made any sense.

Josh interrupted Maria thoughts, "Hello?" he said playfully.

"Oh, sorry." she said, "I guess I was lost in thought."

"Penny for them?"

"No, I think I'll keep them to myself until the price goes up." she replied with a laugh.

"Then how about a dance." he said, extending his arm to her.

"Sounds wonderful." she replied, taking his arm as he led her onto the dance floor.

"You have any plans for the fourth of July?" Josh asked as he waltzed her across the floor.

"None, why?" she asked.

"Well, I know Crytech will be closed for the week. Thought maybe you and I could soak up some Caribbean sun. Or Morocco, if you prefer."

Maybe all this wedding stuff is going somewhere, she thought to herself. Looking into Josh's blue eyes, she answered, "Which ever you prefer. I'm there."

Josh looked up toward the sky as if he was thinking hard, a comical smile upon his face. "Let's do the Caribbean, away from the crowds."

"Sounds wonderful to me."

"Buy a new bikini, buy several." Josh leaned over and kissed her on the neck. "Although I doubt you'll wear any of them very long."

Maria smiled. Six weeks till the fourth and then she would have Josh alone for a week. Just maybe she would be able to get a commitment out of him yet.

Chapter Seventeen

Maria watched as Josh's muscular body emerged from the ocean water. Secluded in a private cove, Josh had abandoned his swim trunks and taken the opportunity to skinny dip in the warm blue Caribbean liquid. Maria, although she now knew that Josh's company owned this land, still felt uncomfortable shedding her suit. 'What little of it there is', she thought to herself.

For the last five days they had alternatively swam in the ocean, dined on fabulous local foods or made wonderfully passionate love. Very little time of their trip had been spent sleeping, so while Josh swam she had availed herself of a quick nap on the warm sands of the beach.

Josh plopped his body down next to hers on the colorful blanket, causing water drops to splash on her hot, oiled skin.

"You look beautiful laying there. Did you know that?" Josh asked, admiration in his eyes.

Maria blushed. She knew she was pretty, but still had a hard time accepting compliments.

"Well, you're pretty much a Greek god yourself." she replied.

"Do you really have to go back tomorrow?" he asked. "Crytech can live without you another week."

"No, I really have to go back." she answered, although she knew regret sounded in her voice.

Josh shook his head. Maria didn't know if it was in jest or if he really was upset.

"Josh, this has been wonderful, really. But I've stumbled across something, maybe something big and I really need to get back and try to figure out what it means. Do you understand? This is very important to me."

"I understand. God knows, I let my work consume me sometimes. So tell me about this thing. Maybe I can help."

"I don't want to talk about it just yet. I may be totally crazy."

"You?" Josh responded laughing. "You are many things, my darling Maria, but crazy is not one of them. I just thought maybe talking about it would help you work through it."

"I appreciate the offer, I really do. But I'd feel better keeping this close for the moment." Maria looked up at Josh. For a quick moment, she thought she saw more than idle curiosity in his eyes. He had never been interested in her work before. Then his blue eyes softened,

"Okay. Back tomorrow it is."

"You could always stay in LA for the week." she said, "I won't be working all the time."

"That sounds good. But we both know that as soon as I'm back in the real world, someone will want my time." he said smiling.

"I know." she nodded, "And if I'm back that means you are too, right."

"That's one way to look at it. But enough of this, let's just enjoy the moment." he said softly as he pulled her close and began undoing her bikini top.

***

After his marriage, Payton and Amelia had purchased a second large country estate. That had been their first battle. Amelia had expected to live in Stone Manor and Payton wanted nothing to do with the place. He knew that when the thirteen gathered in England, then yes, he would have to be in attendance and Stone Manor and that was more than enough as far as he was

88

concerned. While he had no problem spending his father's money, he hated the reminder of the man that the estate brought about.

Unknown to Amelia, he still maintained his apartment over the club in London also. He had found it to be the only place he had left where he could indulge himself without restriction. Here, he believed, he was well hidden from the prying eyes of his wife and the ever-present spy detail of Benedict Enterprises.

As he fingered the glass of scotch in his hand, he thought of how much he hated marriage. He didn't hate his wife, just the thought of being tied down. Allowing himself another sip of the amber liquid, he began to think about the others of the thirteen. Andrew was marrying within the month, and Thomas and Nathan both had plans for fall. He wondered if Josh would ever marry.

In the old days, Josh's line would have been the first to marry. None of the others could until the Christianson male had found a bride. Then would come the Benedict line. Then the others. And none dared have a child until the Christianson heir was born.

Which led to his dilemma now, Amelia wanted a child. In fact wanted many children. He kept putting her off with the excuse that he was not ready yet, when in truth he knew he had to wait for Josh. Josh didn't seem to be in any hurry, although he had dated Maria for years. And who could be more perfect than the sister of the man who had always made Payton feel less than a man.

At times, he didn't know who he hated worse, Josh or Julian. Julian was, at the very least, open and honest with his disapproval of him. Josh, on the other hand, was deceitful. Smiling to his face and yet stabbing him in the back at every turn.

He took another sip and felt the scotch as it burned down his throat like his anger burned his mind.

At the board meeting where he had been given the ultimatum to marry, he had been humiliated in the business sense once more by Josh. Payton had, in his genetic work, developed a fast growing fish, much like the super salmon of the turn of the century. Playing a bit more with the code, Payton had discovered that it too could carry the same mutation genetically that the apples that Joseph Christianson had introduced into the food supply.

Payton had been elated. This discovery would give them yet another way for global birth control. As he presented his findings, he had watched Josh's face. The man had shown no flicker of enthusiasm nor did he even appear interested. When Josh again took the floor, Payton understood why.

Payton had servants bring in bowl after bowl of fruit. Strawberries, peaches, kiwi and many others, all carrying the same properties of the apples. The only fruit not represented were the citrus lemon, lime, orange and grapefruit. Grapes had also been excluded because of their use in winemaking.

Payton had argued that his fish were faster, growing to market weight months before a tree could produce fruit. As always, he lost the argument. The other's had, completely and unanimously voted with Josh.

Payton poured himself another drink. Raising the glass in the air, he said, "One more for the master." That was how he looked at Josh now. Unlike his father, Payton was no longer in charge of his own destiny. Josh and the others controlled him in every action he took.

Only here, hidden away in the tiny apartment could he allow himself to be who he felt he should be. Tipping the old-fashioned glass back, he drained it of its contents.

Picking up the phone on the side table, he waited. When the maitre'd of the club below answered, he ordered another bottle of scotch and a whore.

*****

Josh also kept a secret lair. One only he and Julian knew about. Here they played middle class bachelors. From this base, they would hit the lower end bars and dance halls looking for women who were looking for nothing more than just a good time. They usually found them.

Josh and the young woman entered the front door. "Jules, you home?" Josh said loudly.

The young woman at his side giggled. "He might be sleeping." she said her words slightly slurring on the 's. Josh looked down at her as she looked up at him.

"You really are very tall." she said.

"You really are very short." he replied.

"I'm five three" she said with an attempt at indignant. "That's not so short."

"Who cares about height?" Josh asked laughing. "With a package like yours, you could be a midget and I would care." he said, beginning to unbutton her blouse.

"Don't you think we should go to your room?" she asked, looking back at the front door. "Your friend could be home any minute."

"Good point." Josh said. "It's the doorway on the right in the hall. Go make yourself comfortable." he said kissing her on the cheek. "I'll go get us some munchies and drinks."

"Sounds good" the petite woman said as she walked down the hall.

In the small refrigerator, Josh pulled out a bottle of wine and a small basket of strawberries. Reaching for two glass wine goblets, he left the kitchen and went into the bedroom. Here it was obvious, he had no butler. The bed was unmade, and miscellaneous articles of clothing were strewn around the chairs and the floor.

"Sorry it's such a mess," he said, lifting his shoulders up in a shrug. "Wasn't expecting company."

"It's not a problem." the girl replied. "Something tells me you just need a woman's touch."

"A woman's touch, yes, that is exactly what I'm after." Josh said smiling as he sat the glasses and wine down on the dresser. He poured the wine as he watched her strip to just a bra and panties in the dresser mirror. The girl looked over at him watching her and smiled back. "Are those strawberries?" she asked, "I love strawberries. But how did you get them, they're not even in season."

Josh handed her one of the wine glasses, then picked up the basket of berries. "A friend brought them from down south." he said matter of factly. Picking up the other glass of wine, he made his way to the bed where she was already sitting.

"And since you love them, well then my dear, these are all for you." he said taking one and plopping it into her mouth.

He took another and began caressing her skin with the pointed tip. Starting at her shoulder, he allowed the berry to slide down into the hollow of her neck and then further to the rise of her breasts, before bringing it back up and running it around the outside of her lips finally allowing her to eat. After three more like this, he reached behind her and unfastened her bra, allowing it to fall to the bed. Taking another berry, he traced her nipples before guiding the fruit down her flat belly. He used the berry to run the line just above where her bikini underwear stopped before retracing the route up to her mouth. Several berries later, the tiny panties were discarded also and the berry tray was empty.

An hour later, Josh heard Julian open the apartment door. The woman beside him was sleeping with only a sheet pulled over her body. Josh listened as steps came down the hall opposite his room and he could hear Julian in the small kitchen. Moments later, he heard a feminine voice say, "Are those strawberries? I love strawberries." Josh smiled.

He looked down at the petite woman sleeping beside him and began thinking up the excuse he would use tomorrow to get rid of her. Since it was a weekend, he couldn't use work, so he supposed he would have to use a 'family emergency' of some sort. He did know he would never call her although she would be sure to leave her number.

He closed his eyes but found himself too charged up to sleep. Monday he would have to return to 'real' work, or at least put in an appearance at the board meeting at the foundation headquarters. Once that was taken care of, he would be free to play once more.

"I should call Maria too" he said softly. He allowed his mind to conjure up the images of the trip to the Caribbean. "If only she would loosen up just a bit in bed" he thought. He looked down again at the woman sharing his bed, "No, I'll never give this up."

Chapter Eighteen

Maria stared at the pink and white box sitting on the bathroom vanity. A transparent plastic lab glass filled with a light yellow colored clear liquid sat next to the box. She had been putting this day off for a month. Since returning from the Caribbean nine weeks earlier, she had yet to have her monthly cycle. Without even taking the test, she knew she was pregnant. All of the signs were there, morning sickness, tender breasts, tiredness, but the truth of the matter was simply she chose to ignore it. She knew she could ignore the confirmation no longer.

"Here goes." she said to her reflection in the mirror as she tore the cellophane wrapper from the package. Having opened the interior package as well, she dipped the end of the plastic stick into the lab glass and counted to ten. Putting the plastic cover on the tip, she laid it flat on the counter. Within sixty seconds, she had her confirmation. Both little windows showed a dark pink, almost purple line. She was pregnant.

"Now what do I do?" she asked her reflection as she sat down on the toilet.

Josh would have to be told. Would he think that she was forcing the issue of commitment? She wondered, or would he be happy? But, am I happy? She silently questioned herself. She always knew that she wanted children, but now, right when she was beginning to understand the nature of the genetically altered fruit posed, was not the right time. This would mean time off from work. More time than she had, if her suspicions were correct.

She stood up and went to the kitchen. Instead of pouring herself a glass of wine as she would normally do in the evening after work, she filled the wine goblet with orange juice. Abortion, for her was out of the question.

She was not faced with the inability to care for a child, like she was sure her parents had been. It all came back to the work question, she thought as she sipped her juice. In her mind, she had always seen herself as a full time mother. She could not be one of those women who dropped their children off at day care so they could continue to pursue their career.

"What's done is done." Maria said aloud, quoting a favorite saying of her adoptive father. She would have to take at the least an extended leave of absence from work, if they would allow that. If not, she would have to quit entirely. Her hand involuntarily lowered to caress her belly. The child came first. Maria smiled then, knowing that although the timing was bad, deep down she was very happy.

Feeling content, she reached over to pick up the phone. It was time to tell Josh. It no longer mattered to her if he made any promises to her or the child. He had a right to know, his decision of how to deal with it was up to him.

Not reaching him on his cell, she left a message on both his private office and home phones. Now she would have to wait for his call.

"Do I tell him on the phone?" she said, "Or do I ask him to come here?"

She shook her head. She needed to see his reaction, over the phone she wouldn't be able to watch his eyes or facial expression when she told him. For now, she got up from the couch and went to her desk. Turning on her laptop, she began composing her request for leave letter to Crytech. She would turn it in as soon as she had told Josh. Her research would either have to wait or be turned over to someone she trusted.

Josh stood at the penthouse bar and listened to Maria message on his answering machine. He had not planned to see her for at least another week or so, but it was so unlike her to call he felt that he would have to make an exception.

He had no idea of what she had to tell him, but immediately his mind went to the thought that maybe she had been seeing someone else. He had never asked her not to date others, although he felt it was implied that they were an exclusive couple. He had worked hard at keeping his name from being associated with other women, even in spite of the downtown New York apartment he and Julian had taken under assumed names.

He debated calling her back right then and decided against it. First he would have Julian attempt to find out if someone else was involved with her and if so, exactly who it was. The other man, if he existed, would have to be taken care of. He picked up the phone and called Julian.

Three days later, he had his answer. Julian had found no involvement with another. According to his report, Maria went to work and then went home. She normally shopped on Sundays, hitting both the mall and the grocery store in the same trip. Her days at work were long, normally ten to twelve hours each unless she had a social engagement to attend. Those had always been with Josh. According to Crytech, she had taken one vacation in the last three years-that too being the trip to the Caribbean with Josh.

"Any ideas?" Josh looked across the room to Julian after reading the report.

"Not a clue." Julian replied, "Judging from what I found out, my dear half sister is a saint."

"Angel, maybe." Josh said with a grin, "But she hangs out with us, so she can't be a saint."

"So call her. Find out what's going on." Julian said.

Josh picked up the cordless phone from the coffee table. Ten minutes later, he laid it back down.

96

"Wouldn't tell you?" Julian asked.

"No. For once, she was quite secretive. Said she had something to tell me, but that it had to be done in person."

"So when do you go?"

"You heard. I'll see her tomorrow night." Josh replied.

The next evening, Josh stood outside Maria's door holding a large bouquet of flowers. He handed them to her as she opened the door, allowing him in.

"They're beautiful." she said quietly.

"Not as beautiful as you." he said, "You look positively radiant."

Maria lowered the flowers. "Well you know what they say about pregnant women, they have a glow."

She watched his face and saw nothing. No reaction either in neither his expression nor his eyes.

"Pregnant? How far?" he said.

"Two months, maybe a little more."

"How did this happen? I thought you took precautions."

Maria knew now that he was upset. "The usual way, I suppose. While we were soaking up the Caribbean sun. And yes, I thought I was protected too."

Josh looked at her, wondering how he was supposed to react. Her flippant answer told him that she was more than concerned with how he was taking this, than she was about her condition. She would never agree to an abortion, he could see that she was happy with the thought of having a child.

"It will be all right, Maria." He finally said, trying to soften his voice. "We'll get you the best doctors, the best care."

She looked at him in a way that unnerved him. "I've already scheduled with the doctor of MY choice."

she said. "I have no doubt that it will be all right, I just felt that you should know."

Josh reached to put his arms around her and she backed away.

"I think you should leave now." she said. "I need to think. Maybe you do to."

"Maria, I..."

"Just go, Josh. I'll call you when I'm ready to talk again."

Josh made a move closer to her and saw her stiffen. Putting his hands in his pockets, he said, "Okay, I'll go now. But call soon, all right?"

"I'll call when I'm ready." she said.

Josh left the apartment and stood outside the building in the darkness. Maria was carrying his child. Normally that wouldn't matter to him, but he did care about her. In his mind, he considered his options. He knew she was expecting an offer of marriage or at least a full commitment from him. Yet if the child were a girl, it would have to die to her. He realized he cared more than he had thought about Maria. "I love her." he said silently to the night.

He couldn't hurt her anymore than he had hurt her already tonight. He would wait, see if she found out the sex of the child. If a boy, he would marry her immediately. If a girl, he would allow her to keep her child and consider him a louse for the remainder of her life. Either way, the child would want for nothing.

Walking to his car, he used his cell phone to call Julian.

"I need to get drunk." he said into the receiver.

After a moment or two pause, he said, "I'll tell you everything there. I'll see you in a few minutes."

Folding the cell phone over, he slid it back into his jacket pocket and entering his car, started the engine and drove away. Had he looked in his rearview mirror, he would have seen Maria watching him from her window.

Chapter Nineteen

Julian listened quietly to what Josh was saying, every once in a while glancing around the bar to see if the other patrons were paying any attention to the conversation. When Josh finally said,

"What do you think I should do?" Julian looked into his eyes.

"If the child is a girl, she cannot be allowed to have it. You know that Josh."

Josh looked like he had been hit.

"No child other than the chosen child can make a claim upon the thirteen."

"Maria wouldn't do that." Josh protested.

"You are right. Maria wouldn't. But what happens when the girl child comes of age? Is there any guarantee that she would not?"

Josh sat back in the booth. "I had not thought of that."

Julian continued to stare.

"So what do we do?" Josh asked.

"We wait. We see." Julian said quietly.

"Until?"

"Until we know whether it's male or female?"

"I'm not sure she'll even tell me." Josh said.

"She may not be talking to you. Right now, she probably hates your guts." Julian said, then continued, "But she's going to need a friend. And that friend will be me."

"What makes you think she will talk to you?"

Julian smiled. "I'll start simple... tell her what a cad I think you are. Offer to marry her myself."

Josh's eyes widened. "And what if she accepts?"

"She won't. But she will allow me around to be 'uncle' to the child."

"And if we find that the child is a girl?"

"I'll be there for her when she loses the child. Simple as that." Julian answered.

"You've got it planned in your head already, don't you Jules?"

"I do at that, my friend. I promise, no matter what, no real harm will come to Maria."

"And if it's a boy then what?"

"Damn it man, do I have to spell it out to you? You get on your knees and beg her to marry you."

"So why not just marry her now? Then I can be the one comforting her if she loses the child."

"That my friend, is up to you. Your choice entirely."

Josh sat back and took another sip of his drink. He had known Julian would know how to get him out of this mess. If Maria was going to lose the girl child anyway, he wanted to be there for her. He wanted to be the father of her boy child, the next leader of the thirteen.

"Then that's what I'll do." he said emphatically. "I'll go to her tomorrow. Beg forgiveness. If I haven't blown it entirely, will you be my best man?"

"One thing at a time, my friend, one thing at a time. You've got to get her to say yes first."

Josh smiled. "I can do that, I know I can."

***

Payton sat in the living room of the house Amelia had chosen. While he had been consulted on furnishings, he could see none of his suggestions implemented in the room he was in now. Just like with the thirteen, he was being ignored in his own home. They had just returned from a charity event, one that Amelia had insisted he attend. In the last month or so, those insistences had become more often, many times more than four a week.

Payton hated each and every one of them. Knowing that Julian had been watching him and his behavior regulated him to boredom at each happening. Once he would have enjoyed drinking the champagne or enjoying a line or two of cocaine, now he didn't dare get drunk or stoned while in public. That was reserved for his apartment at the club.

He smiled at his last stay at his flat. The young whore the matre'd had sent up could not have even been of age yet. Payton guessed fifteen, sixteen tops. For him that had been perfect, as Payton realized he liked his girls young. Before they became jaded with life. Tomorrow, when he returned to London, he would have to tip the matre'd well, letting him know how much he appreciated his last selection.

For now, he poured himself a drink. Amelia had retired for the night and other than a few servants running about, no one was around to watch him. He grabbed an apple from the table, taking a large bite, realizing he had not ate while at the social function either. He finished one apple than another as he sipped his drink.

Reaching for a third apple, he thought of Maria. Knowing her work and her passion for it, he had secretly managed to get seeds from the altered fruit of the thirteen into her lab. His contact had told him that she had found an 'abnormality' with the fruit. Weeks later, seed from other fruit found its way into her work.

Now, his contact had told him that she had taken a leave of absence. He himself, had not seen her for months. Josh had been attending social events alone and when asked about her had assured every questioner that she was fine, just busy with other commitments. Had she stumbled on the truth and said something to Josh or Julian? He had hoped her to be smarter than that, knowing that if either of them thought she could harm them or the thirteen, she would be eliminated.

As he stretched out on the long oversized stuffed sofa, he found himself actually saying a silent prayer that she was all right.

Payton was awakened the next morning by the opening of the French doors of the living room. He watched as his wife surveyed the room. Leaning up on one elbow, he said,

"Guess I fell asleep." he gave her a sheepish smile.

"Guess you did." she responded. Looking at the table in front of the sofa, she said,

"You know, I always figured my competition would be another woman... not a bowl of apples."

Payton looked at the coffee table and saw a stack of at least six apple cores. Only one remained in the bowl.

Picking up on her lighthearted banter, he shrugged, "I was hungry. Besides, they were so good. Where did the cook find them?"

"Oh, the cook didn't find them." Amelia replied. "I did. I picked them up at a roadside stand."

Payton's heart sank. "You picked them up? Where?"

"I told you darling, a road side stand. They had bushels and bushels of them and they looked so perfect, I had the driver stop."

Payton had long ago told the staff never to buy fruit outside the supermarket. He never expected that his wife, of all people, would be the one that would break that rule. But he had never told her. Now all he could hope for was that they were safe... that the apples were just ordinary apples.

"Something wrong darling? You have a funny look."

"Now what could be wrong?" he asked, trying to keep his voice steady. "So what are your plans while I'm in London?"

103

As Amelia went on and on about her plans and engagements, Payton tried to think. There was one apple left in the bowl. It would have to be tested.

Amelia was looking out the window and she finished her monologue. "And I'm thinking about a trip to New York, shopping and all, you understand."

"Whatever you want to do, darling, is fine with me." Payton responded as he looked at his watch.

"Look at the time," he said. "I'd better get going or I'll be late for my meeting." Reaching out and plucking the last apple from the bowl, Payton stood and walked to his wife's side kissing her on the cheek,

"I'll see you when you get back, love. Have a good trip."

He quickly left the room and headed upstairs to dress for the day all the while turning the apple over and over in his hand.

A week later, Payton received the report back on the apples he had eaten. Rather than read them in his office, he took the sealed envelope back to his London flat. Arming himself with a triple fingered scotch, he broke the seal on the document.

He sat down as he read the results. Drinking all three fingers down fast, he reread the conclusions of the document. The seeds of the tested apple were indeed identical to the seeds his lab had tested and passed on to Crytech months earlier.

He had broken the line. Even if Amelia conceived a son, his child would never be able to father the next generation. He had destroyed the thirteen. It didn't matter that the destruction would take place sixty years from now, they were dead just as if one of them died without issue today.

Payton tried to think. Julian would kill him if he discovered what he had done. And he would have Josh's blessings. One of the others had to die, they had to die first before this was discovered. He did not want the name Stone to go into the book as the destroyer of the thirteen.

Pouring himself another drink, he thought about the alternatives. It should be one of them that had not married yet. Matthew maybe? He had never cared much for him, or Bart. Either would do, maybe both. The line would be broken now, and there would never be any stain to the Stone name in the book of lineage, simply because they would be no reason for carrying on the book.

Payton slung the drink back into his throat allowing the liquid to burn to his belly. There would be plenty of time. Time enough to plan everything carefully, perfectly so that there would never be any suspicion of his involvement.

Chapter Twenty

Josh and Maria stood on the same sands that they had vacationed on six months earlier. A local priest reading the vows as Julian stood as best man and also gave away the bride. At six months pregnant, Maria was radiant. Wearing a cream colored flowing tea length gown, she knew it not only accented her dark skin color but also de-emphasized her expanding belly.

It had taken Josh months to work himself back into her graces, so firmly was she convinced he didn't want the child. Julian, acting as friend and liaison between the estranged couple, had worked both sides to bring them to this point.

Maria was happy. Her child would no longer be a love child, but would have a name. A name he would be proud of all of his life. Two months ago, they had confirmed that the child was a boy, and although Maria had really wanted a girl, she did not allow the news to dampen her excitement over being a mother. A girl could come later. For now, she was becoming Mrs. Joshua Christianson.

She had wanted a large wedding, one that she had dreamed about since childhood. Yet, since she had few friends and no family, and because of her present condition, she had agreed to this small, quiet ceremony. Josh had assured her that if she still wanted a large wedding after the baby was born, he was more than willing to renew his vows. And although she knew, she would not insist upon it, that simple gesture was what had changed her mind about him.

***

Several weeks later, the thirteen were back at the table at ENKI Headquarters. Each man had just given a report as to what each individual company was doing. Traditionally, Josh was the last to give his speech.

He stood and looked around at the faces of each man. "Gentlemen, we have success." he stated matter of factly. "The test subjects used by our fathers in the sterilization plan, have indeed been proved to breed sterile children."

Short applause was given, started by Julian. "Now, of course all of these test subjects were in Ethiopia, we have yet to receive the data from the Congo. But from all indications, it has been proven that there will be no next generation of selected Ethiopians."

Payton sat in his chair, trying hard to smile and not appear as crestfallen as he felt. Somewhere deep inside him, he had hoped that the genetic engineering that had been done would fail, not lead to sterility, not lead to his downfall.

"And the reports from the Congo... when will they be in?" Matthew asked, looking down at his papers.

"Well, as you know Matt, their mating is a bit more ritualistic there. The girls are not quite as young as the Ethiopians. By this time next year, all data should be in." Josh answered.

"So we proceed as planned, begin the distribution to other places?" Nathan asked.

"Nathan, the distribution to the world has already begun. Six months ago, we began shipping apples, strawberries and kiwi worldwide to soup kitchens, food pantries, and welfare agencies."

"You didn't tell any of us about that, Josh. Should that not have been an ENKI decision?" Thomas sounded indignant.

"Maybe. Maybe I was hasty. Maybe I was a bit arrogant. I did warn you all not to purchase fruit from anywhere other than a reputable grocery. I assumed that you understood why."

"Yes," continued Thomas, "We did assume something was up when we received your memo. But, I think I can speak for the others, we felt that it was only preparation. To get our households in order."

"He's right." Nathan interjected. "I thought it was just to allow time to break the servants of old habits of buying willy-nilly here and there."

"Well, I apologize if I did not make myself clear. Yes, the apples and the fruit are available in certain select areas in many countries."

"Then how do you know that the 'wrong' person may not have eaten it." Payton could not resist asking.

"The fruit has only been distributed to the poorest of the poor." Josh said confidently, "There is no way that it has found its way into markets that need concern any one of quality."

Inside Payton, rage swelled. Every fiber of his being wanted to scream at Josh that he was wrong. That it was his arrogance that had now destroyed the thirteen. But he held it in, smiling. His revenge upon Josh and the others would eventually sooth his anger.

After many more questions, and a few light reprimands by the others, the conversation began to slow.

"And on a lighter note," Josh began to add as he rang the small bell on the table. He paused as he waited for the butler to roll in the trolley carrying magnums of champagne in ice buckets and glasses.

"I wish you all to share my happiness at my recent marriage to Maria Sanchez and the upcoming birth of my son."

As the rest of the men offered their congratulations, Payton sat back dumbfounded. Finally, he spoke, "And when is the lucky day?"

"Actually, it's a bit funny," Josh began to answer, "The child is due April 1st, April Fools day."

No, not funny at all, Payton thought to himself. April Fools Day was the perfect irony for a fool. He now had his timetable in place. So lost in his own thoughts, he didn't notice Julian watching him carefully.

Payton's discomfort finally ended when Josh announced the next meeting. "Friends, we will meet again the day my wife gives birth. We will have much to celebrate."

***

Maria could not ever remember feeling so fat. At seven months, she had allowed herself every eating whim and had now gained almost sixty pounds during her pregnancy. She didn't know what was worse, her lack of discipline or Josh's habits of tempting her lack of control. Almost daily, when he was away, boxes of special delicacies came in from around the world.

She sat on a new lounge chair that Josh had purchased just for her. Its design made it easy for her to get up and down with her bulky frame and she knew it would be used much in the coming two months.

She was excited about the baby, using much of her time to arrange the nursery in the Christianson mansion to her liking. The remainder of her time, if Josh was away, was spent in study. Still researching and testing the data from the apple seeds, Maria had enlisted another Crytech researcher to send all information to her as the study on the seeds continued. She knew, if her friend was caught, it would mean his job, yet both knew that the seed was not an anomaly of nature, but a design given it by man.

Her goal was to figure out who. The mystery of where the seed had originated still bothered her, fueling her suspicions that these particular strains of fruit were not for the good of mankind. The entire secrecy made her feel that something clandestine, bordering on diabolical, was happening in the genetic engineering environment. She had her suspicions of the what, but she didn't know the why or the whom.

As she opened her laptop for the latest email from her friend, she hoped she was very wrong in the way her research was leading her.

When her eyes could no longer stare at the computer screen, she saved her files, passworded them and shut down the computer.

Turning on the television, she clicked through the channels for something to entertain herself for an hour or so. She quickly stopped flipping, hearing a science report that caught her attention,

"The news from the Ethiopian Health Minister today is they have no understanding of why the birth rate is declining. Although immersed in poverty, Ethiopian officials have never been able to adequately administer birth control to the people. And yet, the number of new births from first time mothers is down for the first time since records began being kept. Many health agencies are trying to discover the cause."

Maria laid the remote down on the lounge. She continued listening to the news in hopes of hearing more, yet nothing else was said during the broadcast. Turning the television back off, she reached again for her laptop and began searching for more news online. Hours later, she had downloaded and printed many different reports, from news and health agencies, as well as statistical data pertaining to that region of the world.

As the morning sun began to shine through the windows of the mansion, Maria was more than convinced that what was happening in Ethiopia was not a natural occurrence, but somehow had been manipulated by man.

110

She sat back against the lounge chair, aghast at the possibilities that her brain was coming up with.

Chapter Twenty One

Julian was waiting as Josh walked into the New York apartment. His face, looking grave and angry at the same time, relaxed a bit as Josh sat his suitcase on the floor.

"Well you look happy this evening." Josh said smiling.

"We have a problem." Julian responded.

"I'm sure, whatever it is you can take care of it." Josh said, "Besides, I'm here for a little relaxation. A little fun. I don't need problems."

"Fraid the fun is going to have to wait, old friend." Julian said solemnly, "Crytech Research has been testing our seed."

"Our seed?" Josh asked incredulously, "How the hell did they get our seed?"

"I don't know yet. But that's not the worst of it."

Josh sat down on the sofa opposite Julian. "Okay, tell me more."

"One of the lab researches has been emailing the data to someone else. It's a blind email. We don't know who it is."

"So what the fuck are you telling me Julian. Someone out there knows?"

"That's exactly what I'm telling you, Josh."

"So question the man, find out who he's communicating with. Hell, find out how much he knows."

"Wish I could do that, buddy. But the man is dead. Killed himself last night."

"Shit Julian. Did he know we were on to him? Who tipped him off?"

"That we don't know either. But someone did. Probably the same person who sent them the seed."

"Did you get nothing out of the man? Find anything in his office?"

"Nothing. He had removed his laptop hard drive, taken it apart and burned the inner contents. There was nothing there to recover. We found the email address only by accident, it was imprinted on another sheet in a pad of paper he wrote it on."

Josh sat back and ran his hands over his face and hair. "Julian, I want everyone working on this. Get in touch with the rest. Tell them all. I want answers. Does Andrew know?"

"Andrew was the one who called me. He was visiting the labs when he saw the data on the screen."

"Where were you when the call came in?" Josh asked.

"At Matthew's, most of us were there planning Matt's trip to Calcutta next month."

"Did you tell them anything?"

"No, nothing, I wanted to talk to you first."

"Get everyone at ENKI tomorrow night. We've got to figure out how much damage has actually been done."

"Josh, that's the rub. It had to be one of us who let it out. I think one of our own has betrayed us."

"I can't believe that." Josh exclaimed. "It's just not possible. We're all a group, we're like brother's-there has to be another explanation."

"I hope you're right old friend. I hope you're right."

Josh stood up and walked to the kitchen where he poured himself a stiff drink, "Care to join me, Jules?"

"As much as I would enjoy one right now, I probably need to keep my wits."

Josh reached up for another glass in the cabinet and poured the second drink anyway.

"Nothing more you can do tonight. I know your people are working on it. Drink. I think we both need one."

Julian took the glass and downed the amber liquid in one gulp. "You're right. Tonight is a good night to get drunk." Lifting himself from the chair, he walked to the kitchen and returned with the whole bottle.

"Now I think I understand why Payton drinks," he said. "He does it when he can do nothing else."

Josh could only nod in agreement.

***

Payton had received the phone call before dawn this morning to be at ENKI by dark. Glad to get away from Amelia's whining about children for awhile, he still dreaded the trip, but knew it was necessary.

It seemed they were all scattered around the globe at the moment. Josh and Julian in New York, Matt in India, Nathan and Thomas in the orient. He was at home, but had no idea as to the whereabouts of the others.

After hearing Julian's end of the call at Matthew's home in New Delhi, Payton understood that Andrew had discovered something in his labs. As soon as he could break away from the rest of the group, Payton had placed a phone call. Using a throwaway cell phone, he called his contact at Crytech Research knowing that he would need to do nothing else. From the balcony overlooking the Ganges River, Payton threw the phone into the dirty water below.

Now they were being ordered to meet. Payton knew why, yet was unconcerned. He had been careful and nothing could be traced to him. He knew Julian would have him on the top of his suspect list, but there was no evidence for him to prove his suspicions.

His bags packed, Payton called for the car to take him to the waiting Lear Jet. Once today was over the thirteen would never be the same again. He smiled as he walked out to the car.

Chapter Twenty Two

Matthew Barrister looked down at his watch, hoping the ceremony would be over soon. As a prominent resident and businessman, involved with India's political machinery, he had felt obligated to be here. A leftover from the English occupation of India, his family had worked hard since the days of Gandhi to keep their position in Indian society. They had succeeded.

As both local Indian and American doctors thanked him for his generosity for the new health clinic they were dedicating, Matt had to smile at their naiveté. They had no idea, that the food they were all eating would be their undoing. The buffet table represented the types of food the clinic, doubling as an aide station, would be handing out to the poor and hungry of Calcutta. Similar projects had been both started and dedicated in various regions around the Indian continent.

Finally, he heard himself being introduced, he stood and walked to the podium.

"Ladies and gentlemen, you give me too much credit... " he began.

Ten minutes later, he finished his speech. Shaking the necessary hands, he made his way to his waiting car. Unlike the others, he abhorred limousines and drivers, preferring to drive his own vehicle. His latest was his pride and joy: a poppy red Lamborghini convertible. Beautiful piece of machinery, he thought as he walked toward it.

Getting inside, he put the key in the ignition. Turning the key, his mind registered a click before the engine rumbled to life. Ignoring the strange sound, he turned the radio on. Putting the car in gear, he turned to look behind him as the car exploded throwing metal and human flesh for yards around the pristine parking lot.

The twelve men sat around the mahogany table at ENKI Headquarters. Every now and again, one would look down at his watch. For the first time in recorded history, a member was missing from the table for an unknown reason. Everyone watched Josh, and to a lesser degree Julian, in hopes to know just how to proceed.

Finally, Josh stood, "Gentlemen, I don't know what to say about Matthew's absence. It's unlike him, but we do need to proceed. We can catch him up when he arrives."

At that moment, the head butler came into the room carrying a cordless phone. Handing it to Julian, he said,

"An urgent call from Calcutta, sir."

Julian barked a hello into the phone, expecting Matthew to be on the other end. As he listened to the response, his naturally flushed face went white.

Laying the phone down on the table, he announced simply, "Matthew is dead."

After a moment or two of shocked, stunned expressions, the questions bombarded him. "How, Why, Who?"

Julian took a few moments to compose himself, "A car bomb. Outside the clinic. Right now that's all we know." he replied, looking toward Josh with a pleading look.

Josh, who looked shell-shocked himself, took over. "Gentlemen, we have important issues to discuss. But they will have to wait. We need time, all of us, to assimilate this news. We will gather again tomorrow, when I hope that we will be able to formulate a plan of how to proceed without Matthew."

Josh turned and left the room, Julian quickly followed, his cell phone to his ear. The others left slowly, one at a time. Not much was said, but each saw the grief in watching the other's expressions, until finally the boardroom was empty except for Payton.

Standing from his chair, Payton walked to Matthew's empty chair. "Sorry old chap," he said in a whisper, "I'm sure you will be missed." Suppressing a laugh, he turned and left the room.

***

Maria had not heard from her contact in over a week. While not truly worried, she was concerned. She needed more information, yet her emails went unanswered. She thought of the many possibilities of why, sickness, vacation, supervisors watching the work. She told herself she would give it another week, before she began to panic.

She was tired of being pregnant. With less than a month to go, she felt heavy and uncoordinated. Although there were numerous servants, she disliked the thought of disturbing them for the little things. Josh didn't understand this and when he was home, had them do everything for her even down to a fetching a glass of water. She had grown up in a well to-do household, yet her mother had insisted on doing it all, and she would too as time went by. While she might keep the housekeeper, all the maids and butlers, at least in her mind, needed to go.

'What do three people need with a staff of twenty?' she had asked herself more than once.

Getting up from the lounger, she walked down the hall to the kitchen. Reaching inside the refrigerator, she plucked a bottle of water from the many bottles of water, juice and teas. Josh did indeed spoil her; everything she could possibly want was always within reach. A part of her enjoyed this indulgence; another part hated it.

118

After the baby is born, she thought, I'll work on making a few changes. Taking her water back to the living room she wondered when Josh would be home. He had left in a hurry two days before, claiming a crisis at one of his offices in the Middle East. She was used to him leaving and being gone for days, but this time had seemed different. While still affectionate as he had his bags packed, he had seemed distracted.

"Is it something very serious?" she had asked.

"No, just the normal day to day meltdown out of control." he had responded with a smile.

"Will you be gone long?"

"A day or two tops," he had replied, "I'll call you tomorrow and let you know for sure."

She was still waiting for the call. It wasn't like him not to call when he said he would, but it had happened once or twice in the past. Her eyes glanced at the laptop as she walked past and she saw the new mail icon in the corner.

Setting her drink down, she clicked the icon to open her mail. An email from her contact was there waiting to be read. As she scrolled down the document, she became uneasy. For some reason, the tone of the letter sounded different, as if written by someone else. She was reading the document a second time when the phone rang.

"Hello?" she said holding the cordless to her ear.

"Hello darling," came Josh's voice over the other end. "I have some bad news for you. Matthew is dead."

Maria sat down in her desk chair. "Dead, how?" she said, her voice slightly choked. Matt had always been a fun friend of Josh's and she got along with him well. Like the others of the group, she considered him family.

"Car bomb." Josh's reply came back.

"Who would do that?" she asked, thinking it a terrible way to die.

119

"We don't know yet. But we'll be burying him in New Delhi day after tomorrow, so I won't be home till after that." he said.

"I want to come."

"Do you think that is wise? Are you sure you're up to it?" Josh asked, concern sounding in his voice.

"Of course I am up to it." she replied. "He was like a brother to me... I want to be there."

For a moment, what seemed like an eternity of silence came across the line. Finally, Josh spoke, "I'll send the jet for you tomorrow. Can you be ready?"

"I can be ready in thirty minutes." she responded.

Thinking back to the deaths of the fathers, she asked,

"Josh... you don't think... " she paused.

"Think what, darling?" his voice sounded soft and consoling.

"You don't think this has anything to do with you, do you? I mean... " her voice trailed off.

"I know what you mean, and no my love, I don't think it was directed at us as a group."

"I'll see you tomorrow?" she asked.

"I'll be at the airstrip waiting. I'll have Julian call you back to give you the times, all right. I've got a lot to do at the moment."

"Josh... I love you." she said simply.

"I love you too, my darling woman. I'll see you tomorrow." the phone went silent.

Maria laid the phone back on the desk. The email forgotten, she closed the laptop as tears for Matthew streamed down her cheeks.

***

120

Josh laid the cordless back on the table, as he looked at Julian. "Maria insisted on coming." he said simply.

"I'll arrange it." Julian answered.

"Do we have any idea who did this yet?"

"Not a clue. No one has accepted responsibility, our informants have learned nothing."

"Maria thought it might have something to do with our father's deaths." Josh said.

"I have no doubt many will make that assumption, as time goes on."

Josh sat on the sofa, deep in thought. Neither man said anything. Finally, Julian stood, "Josh it's time to go."

"I know Jules. The others are probably there waiting already. I'm just not sure I know what to say."

"You'll say the right thing, my friend. You always do." Julian smiled and patted Josh on the back. "You always do." he repeated as he led the way out of the penthouse towards the elevators.

The others were indeed waiting in the boardroom when Josh and Julian entered. Matthew's chair was now covered in black silk.

"Before we begin, gentlemen," Josh started, then picked up and rang the small bell. "I propose a toast in honor of our friend, our life mate and a... " he stopped there, shaken, not willing to go on.

As the porter poured brandies for each man, Josh looked at the faces of the remaining men around the table. When the drinks were poured and each man held his in his hand, Josh looked to Nathan. "Nate, you knew him best of all of us... will you do the honors?"

Nathan, his eyes red-rimmed, stood and gave the beginning of the eulogy he would be giving at the service the next day. "To Matthew, a fine friend." he ended.

After the glasses had been collected and the servants had left the room, Josh began again,

"Gentlemen, we have much to discuss today. As some of you may know, our seed has been discovered at Crytech Research. Andrew assures me that has now been confiscated and destroyed. But the question remains of how it found its way there. Any idea's gentlemen?"

Each man in the room appeared dumbfounded. "An employee mistake?" Bart asked. Several other's offered their opinions, until finally Nathan said, "It had to start with Andrew, who else had the seed?"

Andrew rose and started to argue. Josh seeing that tempers were short, immediately stepped in.

"Andrew never had the seed. His work was with corn and wheat."

"Are you sure of that?" Bart asked, still staring at Andrew.

"I am sure." Julian's voice boomed in the room.

"Then perhaps it came from Christianson Enterprises. Josh's firm would have the seed."

All eyes turned to Josh. He took a deep breath.

"Every seed I have can be accounted for. Every seed, every piece of fruit has been tracked and traced to its final destination. The seed did not come from us."

The men around the table grumbled, each now looking at each other with suspicion. Julian spoke next.

"The real problem, gentlemen, is that someone outside this organization knows about this seed. We have yet to identify this person, but we are working on it. The final question this raises is: who have they told?"

"I say we pull the project." Thomas said. "Pull it and destroy the orchards."

"I think that a bit melodramatic, Tom." Josh said. "I, we, need calmer heads before we make any decisions. I just wanted to make you aware."

Several of the men shook their heads in agreement.

"I think, we should meet back here in a week. I know we will all be in India for Matthew tomorrow, and that would give us all a few days to regroup."

More heads in the room nodded.

"When we meet, we are also going to have to think about the future of the thirteen. This has never happened in history before, so we'll be redefining the future so to speak."

Josh looked around the room at the men. He could tell the enormity of the situation had not truly struck them yet.

"It is agreed then, we will meet back here a week from tomorrow?"

Every man in the room answered back in the affirmative.

The meeting over, Josh sat down in his chair and listened to the others talk. Most were recalling their school days with Matthew, days that he himself looked back on fondly. After a few minutes, he finally stood, nodded to the others and left the room.

Julian for once, not following Josh, stayed and listened to the entire conversation. He knew, somewhere in this room was a traitor. Although he had his suspicions, he had no proof and used the time to watch and listen to each man, hoping for a clue-a tidbit of information, anything that might give him more than a hunch to go on.

When the room finally cleared, he knew nothing more than he had before the meeting. He got up and went back to the penthouse, to find Josh waiting for him.

"Anything?" Josh asked as Julian came through the door.

"Nothing." he replied, shaking his head.

"I still don't believe it's one of us. It's just not possible."

"It IS one of us, Josh. I just have to prove it."

"Well then who? Surely you have some ideas." Josh said.

"Some ideas, some thoughts." Julian responded, "I need something more concrete before I even begin to name names."

Josh shook his head and Julian could see his frustration. "You've got to tell me, Jules."

"Not yet."

"What the hell, Jules, you've never kept anything from me before. Anything."

"This is different, Josh."

"How is it different? Tell me that. How?"

Julian only looked at Josh, unwilling to answer him.

"Do you think it was me?" Josh yelled. "Good god Julian, am I one of your suspects?"

"We are all suspects, Josh. Even me."

"Even you?" Josh asked, "How could it have been you."

"Not me personally. No." Julian answered, "One of the company, I don't know. I'm investigating everyone."

"Everyone?"

"Every employee of every company ENKI owns. From the members of the thirteen down to the lowest janitor. Even house servants. I will find out who is doing this, Josh."

Josh sat down on the leather couch.

"I know you will. I still think you know more than what you are saying, but I'll allow it."

Josh said this with exasperation in his voice. "Damn, I am tired. I'm going to try and get some rest."

"Maria will be in New Delhi around eight tomorrow evening. Our plane leaves here at four." Julian said, as he reached for a stack of files lying on a desk.

"Thank you, Jules. For taking care of all this."

"Just doing my job, Josh, just doing my job."

Josh left the room walking toward the master bedroom, Julian went to the kitchen, poured himself a glass of juice. Returning to the living room, he began going through the files on the desk.

***

Once the meeting was over, Payton unlike the others, immediately left Jerusalem. Having his hotel room already booked in New Delhi, he felt had been a stroke of genius on his part. Checking into his room, the first thing he did was avail himself of the mini-bar. Payton had been cautious in his drinking the last few weeks, knowing he needed a clear mind to set all his plans into place.

For Payton, everything at today's meeting had fallen in line like dominoes. Until today, he had been unsure who would be next. After Bart had accused Andrew of leaking the seeds to his researchers, Payton had known exactly who his next victim would be. And who would be looked at with suspicion.

The small bottle of scotch from the mini-bar gone, Payton called room service and asked for another larger' bottle.

"I have much to celebrate tonight." he said aloud to no one.

Tomorrow would be the first time Payton had seen Maria since she had married Josh. He imagined she would be just as elegant and beautiful pregnant as she had been before. He looked forward to seeing her now, if only to inwardly strut at the fact that her child would have nothing to carry on.

After room service had delivered his bottle, Payton sat down to think. The next death would have to be very different than Matthews. An accident in the home maybe, or possibly a mugging gone wrong.

"I'd like to blow his brains out myself." he thought, knowing that would be impossible. When it happened, he would have to be in the company of at least one other member of the thirteen. But not Andrew, as the possibilities rushed through his mind, he tried to determine the best way for Andrew to be blamed. That would take all suspicion off him, and another of the thirteen would fall in the process.

Payton smiled. His mind still wasn't satisfied. He wanted Josh. He himself wanted to be the one to put a bullet in the man's heart. Ah, but to break it first.

From the depth of his mind, the answer came. 'Kill the child.' Payton laughed aloud. So very simple. Kill Maria and the child before he killed Josh. Then the arrogant bastard would know, beyond a shadow of doubt that the thirteen was over.

"Perfect." he yelled into the empty room. "Fucking Perfect." Payton reached for another drink knowing that, at last, his plans for revenge were complete.

Chapter Twenty Three

Each member of the thirteen sat in the first rows on either side of the small chapel during Matthew's memorial service Although a casket sat in the front of the chapel, it was empty as there was nothing of Matthew's body to bury. The only family members to attend, was his mother and grandmother as, like the others of the thirteen, he had no brothers or sisters. The two matriarchs sat on either end of the empty casket. The wives of the thirteen men who had married sat behind them in the second rows.

Each man in turn, took his time at the podium. Each giving small recollections and remembrances of the man who had been their lifelong friend. Most were visibly shaken. After the twelve men had finished, others took their turns. Business associates, secular friends and servants alike gave their eulogies to the man that they had known. Matthew's mother cried openly throughout the entire service.

Josh had arranged for a small reception, or wake, at a local villa. More to protect the now frail looking Barrister women, than anything else. Matthew had always been a man who valued his privacy and Josh had seen no reason to allow strangers to traipse throughout his house. Many at the service had come out of curiosity, wanting and hoping to find out more about the wealthy aristocrat that had lived in their midst. Outside both the chapel and the villa, the media watched and waited, hoping for any tidbit that could be fed to the news outlets.

Julian's men made sure that neither the woman, or the remaining thirteen and their families were captured by either the curiosity seekers or the news hounds.

Maria's feet hurt. Wearing heels and being pregnant, just did not go together she thought amusingly to herself. At the very least, she had found something to smile about today, even if it were her own pain. Within ten minutes of arriving at the villa, she had found an overstuffed chair to lower her body into, and she refused to leave it. Before sitting, she had made sure to find Matthew's mother and grandmother to offer her condolences. She could see in the older women's eyes, that they too felt fear.

As much as she wanted to, she didn't broach the subject of who might have been behind the car bombing. There was already enough speculation about that among the other guests at the wake. Every now and again, she would hear catches of conversation around her, most dealing with the sadness of Matthew's untimely death, but many were whispered gossip of how he had died.

She spotted Andrew coming toward her and smiled. It would be good to see her old boss again.

"You're all alone, my dear Maria." he said as he approached, "Where is that husband of yours?"

"He's around somewhere, Andrew." she answered, "It seems like forever since I saw you last, how have you been?"

"I've been well. But I've got to tell you, between this and Everette's death, I'm really tired of funerals."

Maria was stricken. Everett Stark had been her best research partner.

"Everette's dead?"

"Oh my, I don't suppose Josh had mentioned it. Maybe I shouldn't have."

"What happened? An accident? He was so young." she asked.

"No, it wasn't an accident." Andrew replied, looking uncomfortable. "He killed himself, Maria. Right in the lab."

"But why?" Maria asked, still not believing he was gone.

"We don't know why. He didn't leave a note. No clues, no nothing."

"I just don't understand... " Maria began, then her voice trailed off, as she saw Josh approaching.

"Andrew, good to see you." he said as he reached Maria's side. He looked down at his wife, "How are you doing, Darling?"

"I'm fine." she answered. "Andrew just told me about Everett. So sad."

"I was going to tell you tonight at the hotel. I know he was your friend as well as your assistant."

"Yes, he was. I'll miss him." she said.

"Are you tired, love? Would you like to go back to the hotel? I'm sure that everyone would understand."

Maria was quiet for a moment before she answered. "Yes, I would like that. Let me go make my apologies to the family."

"I'll take care of that." Josh answered. "Don't worry about it. I'll be back in a minute, let me go have the car brought around."

Andrew stayed with her when Josh left. "So you still plan to be a full time mother?" he said with a smile. "We do miss you around the lab."

"Fraid so." she said smiling back, touched that he would offer her old job back to her. "By the way, when is Everett's funeral?

"I'm sorry Maria, it was yesterday."

"Really?" her voice held a question. "When did he die?"

"Last week, Wednesday I believe." Andrew again looked uncomfortable.

"Oh, don't look so glum, Andy. Josh was just trying to protect me not telling me about it. I swear he thinks I'm so fragile sometimes."

Before Andrew could reply, Josh was back. "The car is waiting, I'll walk with you." he said.

Maria stood and hugged Andrew. "It was good seeing you again, boss." she said with a smile.

"You too, Maria. Like I said, you're welcome to come back anytime."

Back alone at the hotel, Maria wished she had brought her laptop. She was sure that her last email from Everett had been after Andrew said he had died. Had someone discovered what they were researching? She wondered. Even worse, did they know that she was involved? Maybe she should talk to Josh. Her mind immediately responded to her silent question with NO. Julian maybe? Another no swelled from her subconscious.

Since it was too late to attend the funeral, she decided when she returned to Los Angeles, she would take Everett's wife to lunch. The two women had always got along, and Maria felt that maybe from her she would be able to get some answers. Deep in her mind, she knew the seed had to be the cause of the suicide. Allowing her emotions to run, she even wondered if he had actually killed himself or if something more sinister was in place.

Knowing there was nothing she could do half way around the world, and not wanting to allow herself to panic over what might be nothing, Maria decided that a warm shower would help her relax and if the child inside her was co-operative, maybe even take a nap before Josh returned for the evening.

Back at the wake, Andrew apologized to Josh for telling Maria about the suicide.

"No matter," Josh had responded, "I was going to tell her, if not tonight, then eventually."

"She just seemed so shaken..." Andrew began.

"Well, they did work closely together for a number of years. I think she, at one time, was fairly close friends with his wife." Josh answered, pausing as if deep in thought. "You know, maybe we can use this."

"How so?" Andrew asked.

"I'm sure Maria will call his wife when she gets back. Maybe she'll learn something we don't know. A few gentle questions and I'm sure she'll tell me the whole conversation."

"You think the wife knows something."

"Probably not, but I don't suppose Maria can do any harm asking."

Returning to Los Angeles the day after the funeral, Josh stayed home only two days before he was off again.

"You do realize this baby is due in less than four weeks?" Maria had said jokingly.

"Why do you think I'm working so hard?" Josh had answered, "I'm definitely going to take a week or two when he arrives in our world."

"Only a week or two?" Maria responded laughing. "You're going to miss your share of middle of the night wake up calls."

"I still don't understand why you won't hire a nanny. I had one. And I didn't turn out that bad." Josh said, trying to keep his tone light.

"We've been through this a dozen times or more, " Maria said, exasperation creeping into her voice. "A full time mother does not need a nanny. We have all the help we can possibly use."

Josh cuddled his face into her neck, "But what if I want to whisk you away for a romantic weekend?"

"Then Mrs. Crawford can watch the child, if need be." she said, knowing that the older housekeeper would be more than delighted to take on the task.

"Okay, okay, I can see I've been beaten." Josh said with a laugh.

"Let that be a lesson, Josh-don't mess with a mama." Maria replied, now laughing also. 'Wait till he finds out I have no intention of sending this child to

Ashleigh either,' Maria thought, 'that's a battle for another day.'

Josh left soon after and Maria finally had a chance to open her laptop and email undisturbed. She had been right, the last email from Everette had come two days after his death. Now she understood why the tone had seemed wrong to her, it had not come from him at all.

Exhaling a deep breath, she was grateful that she had used a blind email account to receive the data. Using an ISP on a foreign server under a false name had been a good idea. As she read through the email, she wondered if she should answer and decided against it. Burning all the information on her hard drive to a CD ROM, she reformatted the drive. Once the operating software was reinstalled, she went online to buy a new drive. Clicking on express shipping, the drive would arrive the next day and she would destroy the existing one.

She stood and looked around the room, trying to determine the best place to hide the CD's. After thinking about it for a few minutes, she went to the wall and pulled the picture of Josh's mother off its hanger. Turning the picture over, she taped the paper envelopes holding the CD's to the back of the portrait and rehung it on the wall. The paperwork she would have to burn. Most of the data was memorized, so it would be no big loss. What wasn't in her memory could be referenced from the CD-ROMs. Turning the gas logs on in the fireplace, she slowly began adding the papers.

Satisfied now, that she had destroyed and hidden all evidence she had of the genetic mutations, she picked up the phone, called Claire Stark, Everette's widow, and arranged for lunch the next day.

Chapter Twenty Four

Payton leaned back against the pillows of his bed in the London flat. A young girl, probably no more than fourteen, lay knocked out beside him. Lately Payton found that roughing up women pleased him not just sexually, but also psychologically, giving him a feeling of power. He loved watching the girls cower after his first strike and watching them begin to beg after the second.

Normally things didn't go quite this far and the girls, after sex, would leave under their own power. He always gave them more than enough money to keep their mouths shut, but as yet, none had returned for a second visit.

He looked down at the young girl. Reaching over, he felt her neck to make sure there was a pulse. She wasn't dead, he thought, as his fingertips touched a strong beat in her neck. He was undecided whether to allow her to wake up and leave or call the matre'd and have him take care of the matter. After a few moments thought, he picked up the phone.

Within minutes, two men had arrived at the flat door and after getting the girl dressed, carried her out. Moments later, a maid arrived to change the bedding. Payton waited as she finished her task, pouring himself another drink in the process. When the flat was empty once more, he picked up the bottle and sat down on the living room divan, wondering what it would feel like to actually kill one of the girls. Somewhere, in a sober part of his mind, the words "Not smart, Payton" came to his consciousness.

Payton leaned back on the divan. So far, everything was going according to plan. He couldn't mess up now, he had too much invested. He would wait, until all was done, then yes, he thought, then yes, he would take a life with his bare hands. The thought thrilled him and he felt himself get another erection just thinking about it.

"Down boy." he said looking down at his crotch. He poured himself another drink, tipping it back and downing it in one gulp. Bart was next, that would happen in the next week or so.

He poured another drink. Then Maria. Pretty lovely Maria. And the damnable child she carried within her.

"Too bad, she didn't choose Julian." Payton said aloud, knowing that if she had, she wouldn't have to die.

"She did not choose wisely." he said laughing, quoting a favorite line from a movie.

***

Maria arrived early. She had eaten at this small, intimate Mexican restaurant many times with her parents. She knew not only all the waiters, but the kitchen help also. Inside, she asked Jose for a table in the corner, out of the way, knowing that she would never be able to squeeze her large belly into a booth.

After sitting down, a waiter came by asking if she wanted something to drink. She ordered an ice tea as he sat two menus down on the table. She didn't need to open the menu, knowing every item on it and knowing that both her and the baby would have heart-burn later that evening. She shrugged as the waiter returned with her tea, a bowl of chip and two kinds of dipping sauce. She casually dipped a chip into the cheese sauce as she waited for Claire to arrive.

"Sorry, I'm late." the younger woman said, as she seated herself at the table. "I got lost."

"You're not late, I'm early." Maria said with a smile, "And yes, this can be a difficult place to find."

134

Maria watched the woman relax. "So, really, how are you doing?" she asked.

"It's been tough. They say that Everett breached security. They're saying he gave, or sold company secrets." the young woman looked close to tears.

Maria looked around the room to see if anyone was paying attention to the conversation. For the moment, they were the only ones in this part of the restaurant.

"I'm sure that's not true," Maria said, "I know Everett, he wouldn't have done anything like that."

"I know. It's just been awful. An investigation team even came to the house. Went through everything, looking at every bit of paper."

"An investigation team? From Crytech?" Maria asked in amazement.

"No, wait a minute," she said as she reached into her purse and pulled out a business card, "Benedict Security Forces... at least that's what the card said." She handed the card to Maria.

Maria looked down at the card. Why was Julian involved in this? She wondered to herself. A favor to Andrew, maybe? She didn't know, but she felt a chill go up her back. Claire was looking at her expectantly,

"I'm sure it will all be all right. There's nothing they could find, right? Everett would never do anything like they are suggesting."

The younger woman took a deep breath, "Then why did he kill himself? Why did he destroy his hard drive before shooting himself in the head?" the agony in the woman's voice was almost more than Maria could bear.

"I don't know Claire, I just don't know."

The woman across the table, took a deep breath and worked to compose herself. "I'm sorry, Maria. I shouldn't have dumped this on you. I'm just so overwhelmed by it all."

"That's not a problem, Claire. That's what friends are for." she said smiling. "How's Tina doing?" Maria asked, knowing the two year old was to young to really understand what was happening.

"She keeps asking about her Daddy. I don't know what to tell her. She's with my parents now, while I work through this mess."

"I'll help anyway I can. You do know that, don't you?" Maria asked.

"I know. But I don't know what you could do. I don't know what anyone can do."

The waiter came back to the table, ready to take their orders. Maria signaled for him to come back later.

Claire had taken the break to compose herself once again, "Enough about me and my problems. How are you doing? How much longer?"

"I'm doing fine," Maria answered with a smile, "Three weeks is what the doctor says. Personally I hope it's early."

"It's been so long since I've talked to you. Do you know what it is yet?"

"They tell us it's a boy. My intuition says a girl, in spite of what they say."

"You really want a girl, don't you?" the younger woman smiled.

"I do. Josh is so happy it's a boy, it would be such a disappointment to him if it's not."

"He'd get over it. Ev felt the same way, until he held Tina in his arms the first time. All thoughts of a boy where gone then." the woman looked at her with a bittersweet smile. "We were going to try for another this year."

Maria tried to turn the conversation back to more pleasant subjects. After the meal was finished, she walked with Claire outside to her car. Scribbling her cell phone number on a sheet of paper, she handed it to the young woman.

"Anytime you need to talk, call me. Day or night. Promise?"

"You may get some wacky calls in the middle of the night." Claire said.

"That's okay. It will be good practice for the baby then." Maria hugged her friend. "Just call if you need to."

The younger woman opened her car door and got inside, "Maria, thank you."

"Like I said, that's what friends are for."

The younger woman closed the car door and started the engine. Maria walked over to the curb, pressing a button on her cell phone. Within minutes, a car came around the corner and stopped at the curb. After settling herself in the back, she thought about the things Claire had told her. Another chill went up her spine, as the baby kicked inside her.

'What have I done?' she thought. 'Am I responsible for Everett's death?' For the remainder of the ride back to the mansion, she tried to convince herself that she wasn't. As the car pulled into the long drive in front of the house, she remained unconvinced.

***

Josh met up with Julian in a Singapore bar. Over drinks, they talked not only about Matthew's death, but also who the contact person was that Everette Stark had been emailing.

"We traced the account back to a German ISP." Julian said, "A woman using the name of Selma Jordan opened the account more than ten years ago. Nothing more than an email account. Paid thru a German bank under the same name."

"Nothing more than that?" Josh asked.

"The bank account was opened with the equivalent of ten thousand dollars. The email account and access cost ten dollars a month. No other deposits or withdrawals have ever been made."

"And the email you forged, was it answered?"

"It was picked up, but no, never answered." Julian said, "We're still working on it. A thorough search of names has come up with fourteen Selma Jordan's. We've checked them all, not who we're looking for - most were little old ladies."

"An alias, then?" Josh said.

"Has to be. We've gone through everything of Stark's, can't find a damn thing. His wife's no help either. She had no clue what he really did for a living other than he 'worked at a lab'. Typical air-headed valley girl."

Josh shook his head. "I'll see what Maria found out tomorrow when I get home."

"You'd better tread lightly there, Josh. Maria's no dummy, she'll know if she's being grilled."

"That she will. Don't worry, I'll just get her to talk, I'm sure she'll open up."

"Like I said, the woman is an air-head, she probably didn't say anything more than "What am I going to do now?"."

"You're probably right. But we'll see. Anything more on the Matthew situation?"

"No one has yet to take responsibility for that. No group, no loner, no nothing. We are looking at a Pakistani national - he had an altercation with Matthew several weeks before the bombing. But there's nothing conclusive - other than the Pakistani's hate for the Indians."

Julian's face looked tired, Josh could tell he had done without many hours sleep. "You need some rest, Jules. Get a good night sleep and we'll talk more tomorrow."

"Sleep can wait until I get this figured out. For now, that's my top priority."

Josh sipped his drink and looked around the room before looking back at Julian.

"Do you think they're related, Jules? Matthew and the invisible spy?"

"I'm looking at that angle too, but I don't think so." Julian shrugged, "That would almost be too much wouldn't it?"

"Indeed it would, Jules. Is this all an inside job? Tell me what you really think."

"I don't know. My gut says that it is, but I have no way of proving that yet."

"And you think you know who's doing it?" Josh asked.

"I thought I did, but now I'm not so sure." exasperation sounded in Julian's voice. "Josh, I've got to ask... what about the thirteen now? With Matt's death, where does that leave us?"

Josh looked at his friend, his face blank. "I really don't know Jules. I'm calling the remainder of us to ENKI next week. I'm hoping by then, I've come up with something."

"You will, my friend. You'll do it and at the same time do what's best." Julian answered, then stood. "For now, I'm going to go try and catch an hour or two of sleep."

"I'll see you in the morning, then?"

"Bright and early." Julian said before throwing a few bills on the bar. "Get some sleep too, Josh. You're going to need it."

"I will." Josh said as he ordered another drink. When he turned back to the stool beside him, Julian was already gone.

***

Payton saw the embossed envelope sitting in the tray on the sideboard in the foyer right after he walked through the front door of the estate house. 'Another damned meeting.' he said to himself. Why the hell, they can't just call in this day and age was beyond him. Every one of them had private cell phones, but no, all calls for attendance at ENKI came on the same heavy vellum stationary that had been used for centuries.

Payton ripped the envelope open. The meeting was scheduled for next Thursday, a week from now, he thought. I wonder what would happen if one of us couldn't be there-sent back an RSVP saying it wasn't convenient. Josh would probably send Julian to physically haul a person there, that's what, his mind supplied the answer.

Several of the thirteen were due to be at Bart's home in Vale this weekend for an elk hunt. Bart an avid bow hunter since childhood, staged the hunt every year in late February. This year he had planned it earlier due to Matthew's death, thinking they all needed a break from day to day responsibilities and give themselves a chance to regroup their emotions. Payton had sent his regrets, saying he would be unable to attend due to prior commitments.

Going into the drawing room of the house, the only room Amelia had let him furnish himself, he poured three fingers of scotch in a glass. Where normally he would have downed it in one gulp, he only allowed himself a small sip. He had been watching his drinking carefully over the last few months, never allowing himself to get drunk while in the company of anyone that could report his actions to either Josh or Julian.

He sat down on the divan and tried to figure out the logistics of Bart's upcoming demise. He knew the when and where, what still needed working out was the how. Both the how of the death and the how of how he could be in two places at the same time. He couldn't afford to make this death as simple as Matthew's had been. This time it had to be something completely different. Something that appeared more of an accident, than a murder at first glance-only later determined to be something else.

A few hours later, Payton rewarded himself with another drink. He had his plan. Every member of ENKI had keys to the lodge in Vale. He wondered why it had taken him so long to see the answer, it was simple. Payton smiled as he sipped the scotch. In the hallway, he heard his wife come through the front entrance.

"I should go tell her I'll be more than happy to escort her to the charity ball on Saturday." What a perfect alibi, he thought as he went to go find his wife.

Chapter Twenty Five

A stretch limo arrived at the front door of the mansion. The driver, putting the car in park, got out and walked to the front door, ringing the bell. Handing a note to the servant who answered, he went back to his car and waited.

The servant made her way to the living room, where Maria was laying back on the lounger, a book propped against her large belly. The servant handed the note to Maria, who read it then laughed aloud.

"Is there an answer, Ma'am?" the girl said.

"Yes, tell him I'll be with him in fifteen minutes." Maria said, raising herself from the lounge. The girl left the room and Maria followed on her way to the master suite. There she quickly changed into a formal maternity gown as the note had been an invitation from Josh to dine at an exclusive Los Angeles restaurant. Saying he had made reservations at seven and his plane was not due to land at Los Angeles International until six thirty - he hoped that she would agree to meet him.

He had closed the note with how much he had missed her and loved her. "How can I resist?" she said to herself as she slipped her feet into a pair of dress shoes. It was these little things that endeared Josh to her more and more. Where most couples she knew had ceased playing in the romance department after marriage, Josh continued to astound her with his thoughtful nature and romantic overtures.

As quickly as her body would allow, she made her way back to the first floor and outside to the waiting car.

At the restaurant, she found Josh waiting, a bouquet of roses in his hand. She smiled as he handed them to her. "This way, my dear." he said as he took her arm and led her to a small private dining area. A waiter appeared with a vase of water and arranged the bouquet on a side table.

After settling at the table, Josh had asked how she was feeling.

"Tired of being pregnant, ready to be a mother." she had replied with a smile.

"It won't be long now, what is it--two, three weeks?" he asked.

"So says the doctor, I'm hoping for more like one."

"Didn't he say also, it could be two weeks later than that?" Josh asked, humor in his voice.

"I hope not. But yes, he did say that."

The waiter handing them their menus, took their drink order and disappeared.

"How long are you home for?" she asked Josh, hoping that it was for more than a day.

"If all goes as planned, I'll be here for the next week. I have a meeting in the Middle East next Thursday, but beyond that I'm all yours." he said taking her hand.

"Hmmm, a week sounds wonderful." she said, squeezing back.

"So what have you been up to while I've been away?" he asked.

Maria looked down at her belly and giggled, "Not much. Did have lunch with Everett Stark's wife Claire earlier in the week."

"So how did that go?" he asked, "She holding up okay."

"She appeared to be. She's very stressed, but that's understandable."

"Did she fill you in on any details?" he asked as he took a sip of water watching her.

"No, nothing more than Andrew had said already. She didn't understand why he would kill himself either."

Maria realized she had just lied to Josh for the first time and she didn't know why. Maybe it was because

143

Julian's company was involved, maybe because he himself seemed too interested.

"I just feel very sorry for her and the baby." Maria continued. "I told her I'd help her all I can, but really, there's not much I can do."

Josh was silent for a moment or two before responding, "You're going to be pretty busy yourself in a few weeks. I know your nature is to want to help, but from what I hear it's pretty unsavory business. Maybe it's best if you stay out of it."

Maria looked at Josh as if seeing him for the first time. "Josh, that was damn cold." she said angrily. "Claire has been my friend for years and I'm not going to desert her just because of 'unsavory business.' Now she was glad she had said nothing of what Claire had told her.

"Okay, sweetheart. I'm sorry. I didn't mean to upset you. Of course, you choose your own friends. I just wanted to warn you it's a bit messy, that's all."

She looked at Josh and softened a bit. "I know, I get emotional. It's alright. But sweetheart, anytime someone you care about commits suicide-it's a bit messy."

Neither said anything for a few minutes. Finally, Josh broke the silence by saying, "Did I tell you that you look beautiful tonight?"

She smiled at him. "I agree, let's talk about us, not unpleasant things."

The waiter appeared again to take their order. Neither had yet looked at the menu, so Josh asked him to return in a few minutes.

"Do you know how much I love you?" he asked when the waiter was out of earshot.

"Probably not as much as I love you." she responded, happy that the conversation was back to more appetizing discussions.

After dinner was over, Maria feeling fuller than ever after dining on lobster tails and scallops, they walked arm and arm back to the waiting limousine for the ride home. Josh remained light and affectionate for the entire trip.

At the house, after both were changed and wearing more comfortable clothing than the formal dress, Josh excused himself from the living room to go make a private call. Maria was used to that, and didn't think anything of it as he left the room, knowing that many of the people he dealt with were in many different time zones than their own. Although it was near eleven at night, in the Orient the new day had already begun.

While Josh was gone, Maria again thought about why she had lied to Josh about her and Claire's conversation. After a few minutes, she convinced herself that she was just protecting Claire's privacy-that Josh had no right to know what was exchanged between friends. Deep down she knew, but wouldn't admit to herself - that some part of her no longer trusted him. That some part of her wondered if he were involved with it all.

***

Payton had arrived in the United States aboard the jet of a business acquaintance. Renting a car under an assumed name, he drove from Houston to Vale. It had surprised him just how easy getting a false identity had been. All it took was money, and to his mind, not a lot of that.

He had talked to Bart earlier that morning. Bart was due to arrive at the lodge later tonight. That gave Payton plenty of time. Pulling into the circular drive of the lodge and veering off on a small lane that led around back, Payton quickly let himself into the lodge itself.

Going straight to Bart's hunting cabinet, he pulled out the harness that Bart used to secure himself in the tree stand he used to hunt. Julian had insisted on these devices for any of the thirteen that desired to hunt, be it deer or elk. Saying he had read of too many hunting accidents of men falling from their stands, he had insisted that each man have one, and each harness had to be approved of by Julian himself. Payton laughed, the God of Security was his new nickname for Julian.

Reaching for the harness, Payton pulled a thin bladed folding knife from his pocket. Working quickly he slit the stitching between the folded over pieces of webbing, knowing that if any pressure was applied, it would rip and the hunter would free fall. He smiled, thinking of Bart falling from a great height. He had no way of knowing where exactly Bart had placed his stand this year, but he was guaranteed that a fall from the stand was almost guaranteed to break his neck, no matter how low. Payton knew it would be at least twenty feet, more if it overlooked one of the many bluffs on the property that Bart was so fond of.

Replacing the harness as he had found it, he quickly made his way out of the lodge, back to the car and on his way to the Denver airport. Under a different assumed name, he had already booked a flight back to London. As Bart died, he would be drinking champagne and dancing with his wife.

**

Bart, Nathan, Andrew and Thomas sat around the fireplace of the lodge great-room. All drank from old fashioned glasses half filled with Kentucky Whiskey.

"You can't come to a hunting camp and not get drunk the first night." Bart said jovially.

"I agree," said Andrew, "What a great excuse to get polluted."

"Not an excuse," Bart responded, "A tribute to the gods of the hunt."

Everyone in the room laughed. "So are we all ready for morning?" Thomas asked.

"Hell, I've been ready a week," Bart replied, "Came up last weekend to check my gear. I plan to be high in the air by daybreak."

"I may be an hour or two behind you." Nathan said laughing.

"Doesn't matter. The land is stocked with many elk, we will all be successful this year." Bart said, his words slightly slurred from the alcohol.

Andrew looked up at the clock over the mantle, "Well, if I'm expected up at the crack of dawn, I'd best be getting to bed."

"Crack of dawn, hell." Bart replied, "I'll have you awake much earlier than that."

"Then I'd better go too." said Thomas as he stood and joined Andrew at the door.

After both had left the room, Bart looked at Nathan. "Couple of whooshes. You'll stay and drink with me, won't you?"

"You bet." said Nathan. "I could care less about getting an elk, I just wanted to get away."

"So we all did, so we all did." Bart replied.

Several hours later, both men staggered to their beds.

The dawn found Bart already in his tree stand, looking out above the gully below. He had sighted several elk here the past weekend and decided this was the best place for success. Reluctantly he hooked himself into his harness. He hated the thing, but understood the reasoning behind it. Especially after Matthew's death. He didn't know what Josh and the rest of them would do now that the thirteen was broken, but he assumed that was what next Thursday's meeting was about. For now, he readied his bow, laid an arrow beside it and waited. He did not have to wait long.

147

Sighting a male with several females coming toward him on the opposite side of the gully, he slowly lifted his bow. Placing the arrow notch in the string, he leaned forward to brace himself as he pulled the bow back into firing position. Leaning forward a bit more to steady himself, he heard a snap.

The elk lifted their heads from their foraging. Another snap sounded and Bart's body fell over the side of the stand to the rocky face of the gully below. He was dead on impact. His body rolled several hundred feet to the bottom of the gully.

When he didn't return to the lodge for lunch, a search was begun. At dark fall, they found his broken and battered body amidst the rock floor of the small gorge. Andrew wept openly in front of the others, while the rescue team recovered his remains.

Returning to the lodge, Nathan was elected to call Josh and tell him what had happened. After the call had been made, the remaining three again pulled out the bottle of Kentucky Whiskey and got drunk awaiting the arrival of Josh and Julian.

Chapter Twenty Six

Josh was asleep beside Maria when the phone rang. Immediately he was wide awake knowing that this phone never rang except in an emergency. Picking up the receiver, he listened for a moment, then said,

"Calm down, Nathan. Start at the beginning."

Maria watched her husband's face grow dark in the dim lighting from the lamp beside the bed. After a few more moments, Josh hung up the phone. He sat silently on the side of the bed.

"What is it, darling?" she asked.

Josh ran his hands over his face. "Bart is dead."

"How?" she asked, her old fears returning.

"He fell from his tree stand. Him and his damn elk hunt."

Josh rose from the side of the bed and began putting on clothing. "I've got to call Julian and then I've got to go. I'm sorry darling."

"No, it's okay. You do what you need to do." she replied as she lifted her heavy body from the other side of the bed. "Should I call Edgar to pack for you."

"That would be a great help. Tell him I'll need warm clothing. I'll go call Jules."

After he had left the room, Maria pushed the button on the intercom to the servant's quarters below. After telling them what was required, she sat down in an easy chair on the other side of the room.

'This is too much, she thought. Two of the old friends dead within two weeks of each other. Death always comes in threes, her mother had often said. Did that mean yet another of them was yet to die?'

Edgar came into the room after a slight knock. Maria only nodded at him as he went about the chore of packing Josh's things for the trip. She watched at how quickly and efficiently he did his job. Trying not to smile, she knew it would have taken her hours to choose what clothing to pack for her husband. Maybe it is a good thing to have servants, she thought to herself.

Josh reentered the room then. Kissing her on the cheek, he said,

"Will you be okay?"

"I'll be fine," she said. "Call me, let me know what is going on."

"I will. And you take care. I'll try to be back before I have to leave again Wednesday, but I can't promise."

"I know you can't. Go, do what you need to. I'll be fine."

Josh kissed her cheek once more before he picked up his briefcase and left the room. Edgar followed with his bags and Maria was left alone with her own thoughts.

Josh called the next day, saying that Bart's funeral would be the following day. Maria, not knowing Bart as well as she had known Matthew asked Josh to extend her sympathies to the family. Josh said that he understood and that he would not be able to make it back before the meeting in the Middle East. Maria found it odd that she was not disappointed at this news, but rather relieved.

Bart's funeral, as Matthew's had been, was well attended at his home in Morocco. Julian was angry and frustrated that Andrew, Nathan and Thomas had decided to call in a local search and rescue team instead of calling him. Now at the funeral, all of the remaining thirteen found their tempers on edge. When the reception was complete, Julian left first heading for ENKI knowing that Josh would follow. As for the others, he hoped they would not show until Thursday morning at the earliest.

Josh entered the penthouse an hour after Julian had arrived. He could tell from his friend's face that Julian was still fuming about the breach of protocol.

"Jules, they were upset. They had no idea what happened." Josh said simply in an effort to calm his friend.

"They were stupid. They knew better." Julian snorted.

"Yes, they were that. But what is done, is done. We have to make the best of it."

"Do you know that the state of Colorado still has the harness that broke? Did you know I cannot get it until they are done with their investigation?"

"Jules, it was an accident. They told us that. Only an accident."

"I don't believe in accidents. I want to see that harness."

Josh decided to go along with his friend, "Have they said when they will release it?"

"Next week, maybe, if they are done with it." Julian replied.

"Then there's nothing to be done until then."

"I chose those harness' Josh, I picked them out. I was sure they would protect them from something like this."

"Ah, so it is guilt you are feeling?" Josh said.

Julian plopped into an easy chair, "Yeah, I suppose it is."

"You've got to let it go, Jules. It was an accident."

"I'll let it go after I see the harness."

"I've cancelled the meeting tomorrow." Josh said, changing the subject.

"Why?" Julian asked simply.

"Only until Tuesday. I need to think and you need answers. Maybe by then we'll both have what we need."

"Are you going back to LA for the weekend?" Julian asked.

"No. I'm staying here."

"Problems with Maria?" Julian asked.

151

"No, not really. She's very emotional, just hormones I suppose. She's ready for our son to make an appearance."

"I'm sure she is, you didn't fight did you?"

"No, not really. But when I questioned her about Stark's wife, she got real defensive. So I let it drop."

"Like I said, the woman knows nothing anyway. So what are you going to tell her has delayed you for another week?"

"I'll think of something." Josh replied.

"You always do, my friend."

Josh shrugged. "I'm going to fix myself a drink. You want one?:"

"Hell, Josh, I want the whole damn bottle. But yes, a drink will do."

Josh went to the bar and poured them both a brandy. Sitting down on the sofa, neither man said another word as they were both lost in their own thoughts.

The next day, Josh called Maria and said he would return on Wednesday of the following week, explaining that he had postponed his meeting until Tuesday after Bart's death. Maria had assured him that she understood, reiterated that she missed him and would be glad when he returned home.

Julian had left early to return to Vale, Colorado in the hopes of prying the harness loose from the state medical examiner's office. He too had placed a phone call early that morning to one of the state senators and was assured that he would receive any and all cooperation possible.

Josh, taking his coffee left the penthouse and walked slowly to the boardroom using the stairs instead of the elevator. He needed time to think. Inside the room, Bart's chair, like Matthew's, was covered with black silk. Unlike Matthew, Bart had been married and was expecting a child later in the year. It was still undetermined if that child was a boy, so there was no way to know if his line would continue. As for Matt, his line died with him.

Josh had allowed one of the private detective agencies owned by Julian to search for a son of Matthew's flesh. He did not care whether the child was legitimate or not, in fact, he had held hopes that a child would have been found among the lower classes of women. Then the matter would have been simple to solve. Pay the mother and raise the child. The next generation could continue. But no child could be found.

Josh went to the book of lineage and turned to Matthew's ancestry. Reading through the entries for the last several thousand years, he watched for brothers of the chosen male who had been adopted out. Reaching Matthew's father, he found that Matt actually had two siblings-one brother and one sister.

Reaching for the phone, he called the detective agency. Telling them to find these two siblings and find out if either had children. Once done, he turned to Bart's lineage and did the same. If Bart's child turned out to be a girl, he wanted to be prepared.

As he read through the lineage of the others, time passed as he waited for a return call. It came three hours later. Matthew's brother did indeed have children, many of them and several women were now in court seeking paternity judgments for children not yet born. It was more than Josh could have hoped for. Telling the agent on the phone to discretely find out from court records which of these women were carrying boy children. He needed no other information other than the mother's name and address.

Hanging the phone back up, he smiled. If one of Matthew's playboy brother's children were a boy child due after Maria's delivery, the line could continue. Somewhat altered, but still a continuation.

153

Josh left the book lying on the table and went back to the penthouse. Later, he thought, I'll go into the city and see if I can find something more fun to do. I deserve it, he said to himself.

Later that afternoon, Julian called and said he had everything he needed. He sounded grim, but would give no explanation on the phone.

"I'll be in late tonight," he had said, "Wait up for me."

His plans forgotten, Josh wondered what news Julian had. Never had he been so evasive on the phone before, so Josh knew it wasn't good.

Julian slammed the penthouse door closed as he entered the room. He threw the harness across the room. "It's been cut." he yelled. "I knew it was no accident. Bart was murdered, just as Matthew was. And one of our own did it."

Josh rose from the couch where he had been half dozing. "Are you sure, Jules."

Julian collapsed into the leather recliner. "I'm sure. The stitching holding the webbing together was cut. Only the upper and lower stitches were broken. The rest were done with a knife."

Julian rolled his head, every muscle in his neck and shoulders ached. "Josh, my friend, Bart didn't stand a chance. Once he put pressure on the harness, the stitches that remained gave way."

Josh paused a moment before he spoke, "You think it was Payton, don't you?"

Julian looked back at his lifelong friend and replied simply, "No."

Josh was taken aback and was sure that his face registered surprise. "NO?" he questioned, "Then who?"

"Andrew." Julian replied almost in a whisper.

"Andrew, why?"

154

"He was there for both murders. At Matthew's before the dedication ceremony, at Bart's hunting."

"So was Thomas? He was at both also. And he has always questioned everything we have done."

"But, like Bart said, Andrew had the seed. How else could the lab have had it, unless Andrew gave it to them?"

"So you think he's behind it all? But why kill?" Josh asked.

"Bart accused him, remember at the last meeting before he died. Matthew I don't know, maybe because he always stood with Bart on things."

"It doesn't make sense. What does Andrew think he has to gain?"

"Does it matter? All that matters is two of us are dead and we have a traitor in our midst." Julian replied calmly, his green eyes meeting Josh's.

"So what now?" Josh asked.

"We wait till Tuesday. At the meeting. I have a few surprises planned. If Andrew is guilty, I'll be able to prove it then."

"Until then?"

"Until then, we do nothing." Julian replied.

The meeting was scheduled for nine in the morning. Thomas arrived only a few minutes after eight, only to find Josh and Julian already at the table waiting. The remaining eight came in quickly after Thomas, so by eight thirty the eleven members of the thirteen were all sitting at their place.

Josh looked at the faces around the room. He had removed the black silk from Matthew's chair and he watched as each man looked at it, knowing they wondered what it meant.

"Gentlemen, we are all here, so we may as well begin." Josh said, looking down at his watch. "First of all, I know you are all questioning the removal of the silk from our brother's chair. Allow me to explain."

He looked to Julian and then began, "The Barrister line has been preserved." He paused as he allowed the other men in the room to take the statement in. "Matt had a younger brother, a younger brother which has turned out to be quite the playboy-to use the society word. One of his many women is carrying the child that will be raised to fulfill the obligations of the next generation. The child is due in July, the arrangements have already been made for that child to be given everything Matthew had."

Josh looked at each man, as he knew Julian was also, waiting for a reaction. Only Payton flinched slightly at the news, the other's looked relieved. Thomas asked, "And Bart... his line?

Josh looked at Julian, who for a split second looked confused. They had both expected this question to come from Andrew. Finally, Josh answered, "Penelope, Penny, is six weeks pregnant. It is too soon to determine the sex of the child. If it should be a girl child, Bart also has a brother."

"Is he the playboy that Matt's brother is?" Thomas asked.

"No," Josh replied, "Married, with two girls already. From acquaintances, we have learned they are still trying for a boy."

Thomas looked skeptical, "Then what, we just take that child."

"Absolutely. We always do what must be done to preserve the thirteen."

Payton found his voice, "Does that mean you plan to fill their chairs?"

"No," Josh replied, "The chairs stay empty until the next generation."

Payton sat back in his chair, trying to keep his face blank. He had not planned for this. He had had no idea

156

that there were others-he had assumed that they were all only children like him. He tried to remember back to when he was thirteen and allowed to read the book for the first time. He had only read his ancestry, his and Josh's. The others hadn't mattered to him then, or at any other time. As Josh continued to speak about the future generation, Payton closed his mind to what he was saying.

He knew now that the only way to destroy the thirteen completely would be to kill all of the men at the table. Especially Josh. Without Josh to lead, the group would be in tatters. He looked across the table and saw Julian staring at him. He too would have to go, before Josh. Payton knew that Julian would protect Josh with no concern for his own life.

Josh sat back down in his chair, as Julian took the floor. After seeing Payton's reaction, he now had doubts about Andrew's guilt. Instead of confronting Andrew, Julian said only,

"Gentlemen, as much as it grieves both myself and Josh, we have to report to you a very unpleasant fact. Gentlemen, one of you are a traitor. A traitor to the thirteen and all it stands for."

Julian paused, looking into the eyes of each man. Searching for some clue, some reaction that might tell him who that traitor was. Only Payton and Thomas met his eyes in defiance, the others held his gaze briefly before looking away.

"Know that each man here is under suspicion, some more than others." Julian continued. "I will find the killer of Matthew and Bart. I know that man is in this room. You will be found out."

Thomas stood, anger sounded in his voice "Are you saying one of us is a murderer?"

"One of you... has murdered, not once but twice."

"Bart died in a hunting accident, that wasn't murder." Nathan injected.

Julian reached below the table and pulled out the tree stand harness. "Bart's death was no accident," he continued, "the stitching of the harness has been cut. There is no way it could hold up against his weight. And there is no way, the cuts were made by accident."

Josh stood, "Bart's death was murder, just as Matt's was." he said. "Whichever one of us did this deed shall rot in hell."

Andrew finally spoke, "But who? Who of us would do this thing?"

Thomas turned to glare at him, "You had the seed. How did you get it? Maybe you had more reason than anyone."

"I've told you before, I do not know how that seed turned up at my labs. When I found it, I reported it immediately. Are you accusing me of this?"

Julian watched the interaction between the two men. The other men were mumbling, mostly under their breaths the same accusation. "It wasn't Andrew." he said simply.

"How do you know?" Thomas demanded.

"I'll be honest, I thought so too. I told Josh, I believed it to me Andrew. Now, I know it wasn't."

"I'll ask again, How do you know?"

"Because he is not acting like a guilty man. Had you accused me, I would have punched your lights out."

"But you're above suspicion, aren't you Julian. Tell me, who is investigating YOU?"

"I am." Josh responded calmly.

"As Julian said, we are all under suspicion. Our activities of the last few months are all being investigated."

Thomas sat down, apparently out of steam.

"This is a fucking mess." Andrew said, obviously distraught over the entire situation.

"That it is." Josh replied, "And a mess that we will clean up quickly once we have all the facts."

He looked around the room and seeing disbelief and anger on most of the faces, he continued, "Gentlemen, I call this meeting at an end. Nothing more can be accomplished here today. We will meet again, the day my son is born. As is tradition."

Josh turned and left the boardroom, closely followed by Julian.

Payton said nothing, he had enjoyed watching the others turn on one another. They would never discover him, he had hidden his tracts too well. By the time they figured it out, it would be too late, Josh, Julian and the unborn next leader of the thirteen would be dead.

***

Maria had spent hours pouring over data. She had already concluded that the apple seed would be incapable of regenerating itself. No seed from the apple would gestate, no seed would sprout, it lay barren and sterile no matter the medium it was fostered in.

The question that continued to come up in her brain frightened her more than she cared to admit. If one ate of the apple, would that somehow change the human genetic code to sterility? Her rational mind told her that her that this was an impossibility and that she had no data to back up any such hypothesis. Yet the story of the sterility crisis in Ethiopia continued to haunt her that too was an impossibility.

"I'm too much like my father." she finally said to herself, closing the file in her lap. Martino Sanchez had been a filmmaker in Hollywood, known for his beliefs in conspiracy theories, especially those of the Illuminati. For many years, she had heard those theories over the dinner table, as he discussed them with both his wife Carlita and the many guests that came and went in the house.

The baby kicking inside her, she laid back on the lounge and allowed her imagination to take over. What if, she thought, someone had come up with a way to sterilize the world's poor? What better representation of good and evil than an apple, the forbidden fruit of Christian tradition? You're being silly, she thought to herself, there's other fruit involved too-only you haven't researched them as thoroughly. Besides, who would do such a thing? How could they control it. It's just a quirk of nature, she told herself firmly. That's all-an anomaly of the chaos of nature.

Yet now that she had started the thought, she couldn't shake it. What sort of evil would do this kind of thing? She missed Everett, only with his help could she have ever figured out if the two events were at all related. She didn't dare ask anyone else at the lab for help, not after what had happened to Ev.

Once the baby settled down, she rose from the lounge and put the documents back into their hiding places. She didn't understand why she didn't trust Josh with this information, but every instinct she had told her not to. Maria had since she was a small child, listened to those voices inside her that told her what was right and what was wrong.

Looking at the clock over the mantle, she saw that it was well after eleven. Taking a deep breath as she stretched, she placed her hand upon her belly.

"You going to let Mama sleep?" she asked her unborn child. A kick against her hand was the only answer she received.

"Well, little one, I think we'll give it a try anyway. Okay?" she said laughing, leaving the living room, heading for the master bedroom. After getting dressed for bed, she wondered if she should try to call Josh and

160

decided against it. There was no telling what part of the world he was in at the moment and what she might interrupt. Pulling the phone closer to the edge of the nightstand, she climbed into bed and was quickly asleep.

Chapter Twenty Seven

Payton entered the London flat in a dark, depressed mood. Pouring himself a stiff drink, he slammed the liquid back in his throat. Not only was he depressed, he was angry. Angry that Josh had found a way around the destruction of the thirteen.

How he had wanted to protest bringing in Matthew's brother's child, yet one look at Julian's face told him that he didn't dare. He tried to think if he had shown any of his anger at the meeting, but felt he had done a good job of hiding his emotions. Still there was no way that he could be traced back to the deaths.

Maria was next, he decided as he poured another drink. Then Julian... then Josh. Sitting on the leather sofa, he allowed himself to fantasize how to kill each one in their turn. All he knew is that he would now have to act swiftly. Maria's child was due any day and he had no intention of allowing her to deliver.

A smirk shadowed on Payton's face. With Josh gone, who was to say he could not lead the others. They would all be so confused, since they had spent their entire lives listening to and following Josh's orders. Without Josh, and Julian to back him up the remaining eight members would be grateful for someone to take charge and tell them what to do next. It would be his crowning moment, Payton thought. With a cool head, he would be able to kowtow the others easily.

As he thought of the power he could wield, Payton felt his manhood pressing against the tweed of his slacks. Reaching for the phone, he called downstairs, asking for the matre'd. Asking for a very young girl this time, Payton sat back to wait. An hour later, no one had yet arrived and now angry, Payton reached again for the phone. As he listened to the man on the other end attempt to explain why no girl had been found, he finally screamed into the receiver,

"Well, fuck it then." before slamming the phone down on the table.

When he was leader, he would be able to have a stable of young girls, he thought. No one would stop him. He would be able to divorce Amelia and live his life the way he chose. There would be no Josh or Julian looking over his shoulder.

Thinking of Amelia, while the thought of her made his stomach turn, he realized that she could have a part to play in him reaching his goal.

He would have her call Maria, a courtesy call more or less, to check on how she was doing. While they were not great friends, they were amicable acquaintances and this would not be looked at with suspicion. Payton knew it would be impossible to harm Maria while she was at home in the mansion. It would have to be done elsewhere, maybe at a lunch out or to or from a doctor visit. Amelia could find that information out for him.

He knew that now he was going to have to work quickly. If it were all humanly possible, he hoped that they could all be out of the way by the end of the next week. He would have to be careful, but it could be done.

Reaching for the phone again, he called his wife and set his plan in motion.

***

Josh and Julian sat in the tiny living room of the apartment. Neither man said much, as each was lost in their own thoughts. Finally, Josh broke the silence,

"What made you decide it was not Andrew?"

Julian looked at his friend, "Had Thomas accused me and I had been guilty, I would have knocked him on his arse--just as I said at the meeting. Andrew did not act like a guilty man."

"You are right of course," Josh responded, "He looked positively stricken when Thomas accused him."

"That he did." Julian replied simply.

"So now who? Any ideas?"

"Thomas maybe ... Payton."

"I thought you had ruled Payton out?"

"I had, until the meeting. There was something about his expression, or lack of one, that bothers me."

"You are basing your judgment on an expression?" Josh asked.

"He seemed to be enjoying the melee that went on in there. Almost like Thomas and Andrew at each other's throats was a reward of some kind."

Josh merely looked at his friend.

"Jules, you really do not think he could have pulled this off, do you?"

"There is much we do not know about Payton. Like where he goes when he disappears for days. It never really mattered before, but I think now it does."

"And Thomas, why Thomas?"

"He was so quick to accuse. Too quick maybe."

"None of it makes sense to me Jules. What does anyone of them have to gain from destroying the thirteen? I have played this over and over in my mind, and have come up with nothing."

"A feeling of power, maybe? Hell, I don't know. All I know is that I want to find the bastard fast. I want to make him pay."

"Which brings up the next thing I have been struggling with. What do we do with him? When we find him. We still have to carry on the lineage."

"Good question, my friend." Julian said and then began smiling.

"You have an answer, I see it in your face."

164

"A possible answer."

"What?" Josh said, "Do not keep me in suspense."

"If I remember correctly, the Barrister holdings include a hospital outside of New Delhi. If I am not mistaken, its primary purpose is an insane asylum. Whoever our culprit is ... " his voice trailed off.

"Could be placed there for the rest of their natural life. We could preserve the line by having the staff collect his sperm until a male child was born."

"Exactly."

"It would work. It would be a fate worse than death, for sure. Unlike hospitals in the civilized world, life would be very unpleasant there."

"It would be perfect. He would be totally under our control and once the heir was born -- who would care what happened to him?"

A halfhearted laugh escaped Josh's lips. "You are one mean bastard, yourself, Jules. But you knew that already, did you not?"

"I only do what has to be done to fulfill my oath. You know that Josh."

"I know. That is what all of us do."

"All but one. All but one. And I will find out who that one is, I promise you that."

"Just do it soon," Josh replied, allowing another half chuckle. "This whole thing is wearing me down. I should be home with Maria."

"You will be there for the birth of your son Josh, do not worry, I will see to that."

Chapter Twenty Eight

Maria had been pleasantly surprised when Amelia had called earlier in the day. The woman had been warm and friendly as she had asked Maria about the baby. Maria suspected that Amelia might be pregnant herself, as she had asked about the doctors Maria was seeing, the schedule and all sorts of things about the last month of pregnancy.

That would be sweet, she thought to herself. Her child would probably just as tight friends with Bart and Payton's children as her husband was with their fathers.

Maria was still convinced that the child she carried was a girl. At her appointment last week, she had insisted that the sex be tested for again. Josh was so determined for it to be a boy, she wanted to have time to prepare him before she was on the delivery table.

"That is if he comes home before then," she said to the empty room. She knew he had been devastated by the deaths of both Bart and Matt. Knowing that many of their business concerns were interconnected, it did not surprise her that he was busy trying to get everything worked out and in order. He would be here for the birth and if all went well, maybe a week or two after.

If I am honest to myself, she thought, I have not really missed him much. When he was home, other than an hour or so for dinner, he was totally preoccupied with work anyway. On the phone from dawn to late into the night, she rarely spent any real time with him. Once the baby was born, the child would fill most of her lonely hours. She remembered that her own father was gone most of the time on film shoots, leaving her mother alone with only herself for company. 'It is the way the world works.' she told herself.

Maria stood and slowly walked to the nursery. Everything in the room was in readiness for the child. 'Everything for a boy child.' she said to herself. Going to the large walk in closet, she went to the back where many boxes were stacked on the shelves. Pulling one down, she walked back into the nursery and sat in the rocking chair beside the crib. Opening the box, she pulled the still wrapped items one by one from the box. As she looked at each, she allowed herself to imagine each in its place, transforming the room from a boy's room to a girls.

Looking at the white four poster crib, she imagined the blue sheets, quilts, and bumper pads replaced with the light pink ones in her lap. Although the crib had been designed for use with a canopy, none existed now, yet the soft pink netting was in the box also.

Maria sat back as she pulled a delicate pink and white dress from the box. This was what her daughter would wear home from the hospital. Providing her instincts were correct.

"I should not have let it go on this long." she said aloud, "I should have insisted on this retest months ago."

She shrugged, she would have the answer Tuesday when she returned to the doctor. Two days and she would know for sure. Putting everything back into the box and reclosing the lid, she returned it to its place at the back of the closet.

The child in her belly turned and kicked. "Are you as ready to come out of there as I am ready for you?" she asked the unborn child. "You know it does not really matter -- if you are a girl or a boy -- you will be a loved child."

She smiled as she rubbed her belly ... "but you are a girl, I just know it."

167

Payton returned to the estate in high spirits. Amelia had done just as he asked calling Maria. Now he knew what her schedule would be for the next week or so. Amelia had used the pretense of a throwing Maria an after birth baby shower in London for her call. Payton had known when he suggested the event that all he would have to add was 'all gifts are for the poor and underprivileged of London' for his wife to take the bait. Amelia thrived on hosting the most unique charity events and the shower would fit perfectly in her social milieu.

As a reward for doing as he had asked, Payton had made reservations at one of the classiest French restaurants in London. There he would be the perfect husband, allowing Amelia to prattle on about anything that interested her. Even children, Payton said to himself. He knew that the subject would come up and he would tell her tonight that yes, he was ready to try and have a child.

Even though he knew that would never happen, the thought would thrill her and she would be easier to live with until she found herself dumped. Payton smiled and considered having a drink. No, he said to himself firmly, no more until after all his plans were complete. Then, and only then would he allow himself to celebrate.

Leaving the drawing room, he went upstairs to dress for dinner.

At dinner, Amelia was radiant in a light blue formal gown that sat off her blond hair and blue eyes. Payton saw that she was a bit taken aback when he ordered nothing to drink for himself besides water.

"Well, I can't very well drink alone, can I darling?" she had asked.

Afraid that it would get the dinner off on the wrong foot, he had relented and ordered a bottle of wine.

Silent as the Stewart poured them both a glass, he asked when the man had left the table,

"You look more beautiful than usual, darling. That gown does do you justice."

"I found this in Paris last week," she said, "is it not it the perfect little dress?"

Payton was used to the shallowness of his wife. He had found out quickly after their marriage that her charity work was more for how it made her look instead of the cause that she was championing at the moment. She really is a lot like me, he thought, too bad.

As they ate appetizers of raw oysters and escargot, she again brought up Maria.

"She sounded so happy, darling. Having a child and all."

"I am sure she is." he responded.

Amelia was quiet and Payton wondered what was going on in her head, but felt he knew.

"You want a child, do you not sweetheart?" he asked.

Across the table, Amelia took a deep breath before answering, "I am pregnant, Payton. I just had it confirmed today."

Payton stared at his wife, anger welling up inside of him. Finally, he stammered, "Pregnant?"

"I know you are not ready for a baby, Payton, but I have wanted one badly. I promise it will not get in your way. You will not have to change your lifestyle a bit. Neither I or the child will make any demands on you."

Payton continued to stare at his wife. He knew the child was not his -- there was no way. But between someone else's child and the lengthily prenuptial agreement she had signed, it would now be very easy for him to divorce her when he was ready. Payton smiled across the table.

169

"It is okay, darling. I had guessed the subject was going to come up tonight. I was going to tell you that I was ready to be a father."

He watched as Amelia visibly relaxed. "So how long do I have before this blessed event?" he asked.

"Eight months, more or less," she said, "I have only just missed my monthly."

Payton motioned to the wine steward and ordered a bottle of champagne. After the glasses were poured, he lifted his toward his wife,

"To a happy, healthy pregnancy my darling."

Payton ate the remainder of his meal, while his wife prattled on about baby names and nurseries. He only nodded and agreed when necessary to everything she said. His mind was on tomorrow and his flight to Los Angeles.

***

Josh had chosen to return to the penthouse at ENKI headquarters for a week instead of returning home. He would return to Los Angeles on Friday, he had told Maria earlier in the day. Barring any extreme complications, that would allow him to be home for the birth of his son. Julian was due in at any time and Josh was anxious to discover what he may have learned. For the next five days, both men would be working out of the penthouse.

Josh had the latest reports from the Congo in front of him, and as he studied them, he heard the penthouse elevator chime in the hall. Moments later, Julian walked through the door.

"Anything?" Josh asked.

"Much. But give me a minute to catch my breath, will you?"

"Take your time." Josh answered nonchalantly.

Julian took his bags to his quarters, then returned to the bar where he poured both men a drink. Handing Josh's to him, he said,

"Want to hear something that will blow your mind? It is really kind of funny."

"I am all ears," Josh replied, "I could use a laugh."

"Amelia's been cheating on Payton for months. He does not have a clue."

"Really? Who with?"

"Some artsy-fartsy museum director. Did not even stay within her own class."

"Payton will be furious."

"As much as Payton is gone, I doubt he will care. Besides, he has other diversions."

"Other diversions? What a mistress or two?"

"We have found that Payton has maintained a flat above his London club since his marriage. Seems the matre'd has been supplying him entertainment whenever he asked."

"Payton has been fucking whores? Paying for it?" Josh asked unbelief in his voice.

"Worse than that. His latest was only thirteen. Payton is a degenerate, he likes little girls."

Josh looked at Julian and saw the man was not finished yet.

"What else, Jules?"

"He likes to beat these girls, Josh. He almost killed the last one. The matre'd said that other than when he would arrive and leave, he had never seen Payton sober."

"We have known since high school, he is unstable when he is drunk. But how did he hide this -- this secret life?"

"False names, false identities. I found a forger that claims he has made at least four different identities for him."

"Could he be Selma Jordan?" Josh said, thinking about the seed and how it came to be at Andrew's lab.

"He well could be. I have got men working twenty four seven on his alias'." Julian answered. "It should not be long now before we discover the truth."

"Payton is the traitor, is he not, Jules?"

"He is. I should have seen it coming, but I promise, once I have enough proof, he will wish he had never been born."

"Have you got things ready at the hospital?" Josh asked.

"Everything is in place."

"I have taken the liberty of hiring a special doctor, a psychiatrist that comes highly recommended, to work exclusively with our patient."

"Who Josh? Joseph Mengele?" Julian asked trying to insert a bit of humor into what he felt was a bad situation.

"Joseph Mengele would be considered Madame Curie compared to Doctor Aaron Lethgow." Josh smiled, "Look him up, Jules. The man has been barred from practice in most of the world. His nickname is Aaron the Barbarian."

"When does he start?" Julian asked.

"He is already in place. He was more than willing and the hospital was glad to have him."

"So now we just need our traitor." Julian replied.

"The day the birth of my son is announced," Josh said, "is the day we have Payton removed from the boardroom in a strait jacket."

"I will drink to that." Julian said, nodding his approval.

Chapter Twenty Nine

Payton arrived at the airfield early, anxious to get this trip to the United States over and done with. His pilot informed him that they still had at least an hour before they could take off. Payton brushed him away with a hand movement, and boarded the small Lear Jet. True to his word, it was almost an hour before they began the taxi down the runway.

Payton watched from the window as they climbed in altitude, his spirit improving with every foot above ground. Once they were cruising above the Atlantic, Payton began pacing the floor of the small cabin.

He still had not quite figured out how to get Maria away from her driver. He knew, even if she did not, that the driver was an employee of Benedict Security - hired by Julian to be both driver and bodyguard. Once the driver was out of the way, the rest should be easy, he thought.

Something will come to me, he said under his breath. Reclaiming his seat, he laid the seat back and tried to sleep. They would refuel in New York, before making the final leg of the journey to Los Angeles. He still had plenty of time.

***

In his office within the headquarters building, Julian closed the file before him on the desk. Picking up the receiver, he buzzed the penthouse and waited.

"You best come down here, Josh." he said when the line had been picked up.

Minutes later, his friend walked through the door. "What is it?"

173

Julian slid the file across the desk. "There is enough there to hang Payton. And I have only scratched the surface."

Josh sat down in the leather chair on the other side of the desk and began reading the file. He stopped after the first two pages.

"So this, Roger Covington is one of Payton's alias'?" he asked.

"Yes, and Roger Covington was in Vale the day before Bart died. Pierre Blouchette, another alias, was in Calcutta the day Matt died."

"Have you tied him to the seed?" Josh asked. "I still do not understand how anyone could have got that."

"No, not yet and I do not think that really matters any longer." Julian replied.

"Selma Jordan, have you found her yet?"

"Not yet, but we do have a few new leads."

"Nothing conclusive?" Josh asked.

"We have found that the name 'Selma Jordan' was a pen name used by a Radcliff student years ago to report on her summer travels in Europe. We have someone there now, attempting to find out the real name of the writer."

"You think this is connected?" Josh asked.

"We are looking into it. The timing of the campus newspaper articles and the opening of the bank and email accounts coincide."

Josh laid the folder back on Julian's desk. Maria went to Radcliff, I wonder if she would know.

Julian looked at Josh briefly before looking away, saying nothing.

"What?" Josh asked.

"Maria was in Europe during that time also."

"You think Selma Jordan is Maria?" Josh asked, not quite believing what he was hearing.

"Stop and think about it a minute, Josh." Julian continued, "Maria and Everett Stark worked together for

174

years at Crytech. Could she really not have known what he was doing?"

"I do not believe this." Josh said getting up from the chair and pacing across the room. "How much do you think she knows?"

"Not enough to hurt us. But we do need to find out how much."

Josh paced the floor. "After my son is born, we will do whatever we have to do to find out."

Josh looked at Julian, who had a sad look on his face.

"Your sister and my wife..." Josh said, "Who would have guessed?"

"I suppose we should have." Julian said quietly, "I think we both let emotion blind us a bit where she was concerned."

Chapter Thirty

Payton had a limo waiting at Los Angeles International when the Lear Jet set down. Once inside, he gave the driver the address he was to be taken to. As the limo pulled onto Rodeo Drive, Payton scanned the streets, looking not only at the layout of the high class stores, restaurants and office buildings, but also looking for either Josh's Rolls or Maria's red sports car. He saw neither. Having the driver drop him at an upscale outdoor cafe, his eyes searched the street.

Maria's obstetrician had offices located on the other side of the wide boulevard. Next to it, stood a baby store on one side and a candy store on the other. Payton sprinted across the road to the baby shop.

Inside, he dismissed the sales girl with an "I am only just looking." statement as he watched the street in front. Within minutes, Josh's Silver Cloud pulled up to the curb out front. Ignoring the no parking sign, the driver turned off the car and jumped out and around to the passenger side.

Opening the door, he extended his hand to Maria, helping her from the car. The driver then ran to the front door of the building opening the large glass panel for the pregnant woman. He stood at the door as she disappeared inside, and then returned to the Rolls, starting it and moving it down the street to an acceptable parking spot amongst the other limo's and high priced vehicles.

Payton waited until he felt the driver was settled, then strolled down the street to the parking area. Tapping softly on the tinted glass, the driver rolled down the window.

"Mr. Stone. Good to see you. Is there something I can do for you?" the driver asked.

"Nothing at all." Payton said as he pulled a gun from his pocket and shot the man in the head. He watched as the driver fell sideways into the bench seat. Opening the door quickly, he rolled the window back up and shut the door. He peered at the glass and could see nothing.

Walking away, he was confident that no one else would be able to see anything either. He went back to wait outside the doctor's offices for Maria to appear.

Maria was humming as she left the ob/gyn's office. She had been right and the doctor wrong. She carried a girl inside her belly. And the doctor had told her to be ready, she could deliver any day now. She had already begun dilating and they had reviewed the procedures for the when and how of delivery.

All Christianson women delivered their children at home and Maria would be no different. The doctor would be sending a team tomorrow to outfit one of the many guest rooms, turning it from a bed room to a delivery room.

She was excited and could not wait to call Josh and tell him he needed to return home if he wanted to be there for the delivery. She would wait until he arrived to break the news gently that this was not going to be the son he hoped for.

Leaving the elevator, she was surprised not to see the Rolls out front waiting for her. As she stepped to the doors, she was taken aback when Payton opened the door for her. His face frantic, he began stuttering...

"There has been an accident. I'm... I'm... I'm to take you to Josh." Payton said.

Maria nearly fainted at the news. "What kind of accident? Is he okay? Payton, tell me."

"I...I...I don't know how bad it is. I just got the call from Julian. He said to bring you."

"Please, yes," Maria could barely hold her voice steady, "Take me to my husband."

Payton took her arm and led her to his waiting limousine. For a brief moment, she wondered what had happened to her own car and driver, but dismissed that as unimportant. Payton said little in the car, and could not answer any of her questions.

"Where are we going?" she asked as the limo turned at the airport exit.

"Jerusalem." Payton answered, "That is where Josh is."

"I do not have my passport." she said absently, just to fill the air with words.

"Not to worry. I have the private jet. You will not need it."

"Oh." she replied, thinking that strange, yet too worried about her husband to care.

Aboard the jet, Payton seemed agitated. Maria wondered if he knew something he was not telling her and yet was too wrapped up in her own thoughts to ask. Little was said on the trip to New York for refueling other than she did ask how long the trip would be.

"At least ten hours." Payton had replied, "Why do you not try and get some rest?"

Maria lay back in her seat, closing her eyes as the baby kicked wildly inside her. She awoke hours later to find herself somewhere over Africa.

"We will be landing in an hour or so." Payton said, "Can I get you anything, water? Tea?"

As she lifted her seat upright, she responded, "Water would be nice."

"Would you like something to eat?" Payton asked soothingly "It has been a long trip and I do not know when you'll get another chance."

"I do not know," she replied, taking the drink from his hand.

"I have cheese and fruit." Payton smiled at her.

"Do you have crackers? Cheese and crackers would be good. I have never been a fruit eater."

"Cheese and crackers it is, then." he said as he returned to the small kitchenette at the side of the plane.

***

Josh had spent hours since he had talked with Julian attempting to work. His mind would not focus. All he could think of was Payton, Maria and how everything had gone terribly wrong.

They were going to rule the world, this generation of the thirteen. No one could stop them, they had the money, the connections, and the power needed to do whatever they pleased and no one could have stood in their way. Except one of their own.

He should have seen it coming, he thought as his mind went back to Payton's first day at boarding school. From day one, the younger boy had been a whiner always unwilling to participate with the others unless he saw that he had something to gain.

After Payton's initiation, Josh remembered how he had returned to school, puffed with pride and arrogance over who he was. Shortly after that was when he had begun drinking. With each drinking episode, he had become more insolent with the others and other than school mandated events, had reached the point where he shunned everyone.

'Forgot about that.' Josh said to himself as he allowed more memories to flood his mind.

One humorous one came to mind as he thought about the last rugby game before he had graduated and gone off to college. Josh had invited Payton to play and to his credit, Payton had delivered a very memorable line,

"I go out of my way to avoid things that cause me pain," the younger man had said, raising a beer bottle in the air, "except for drinking."

If only they had realized then how drinking would come to rule Payton's life in the future. Maybe they would have been able to do something, anything, to change the events that were happening today.

But he had truly believed that when he and Julian had returned to the school two years later to cover Payton's crime, that they had solidified his trust in them.

"How wrong we were." Josh said to no one as the room was empty.

And Maria, he thought. Something must be done about her also. Even though Julian was convinced that she would never be able to put everything together, she knew too much. But that was a decision that would wait ... would wait until after the birth of his son.

Without knocking, Julian came into Josh's private office, his face grim.

"We have got problems."

"What now?" Josh asked totally exhausted.

"Maria's driver is dead, and Maria is missing."

Josh closed his eyes, allowing his mind to take in the information.

"There is more." Julian said, his voice slicing the air.

"What more?" Josh asked, hoping fear did not sound in his voice.

"We cannot find Payton either."

"Oh, fuck." was all that Josh could reply.

"Josh, I have every man available looking for her. And for him. We will find them."

"You think Payton has Maria?"

"It makes sense."

Josh paced across the room. Finally, he stopped at the office door. "I am going for a walk. I need to think -- to get out of here -- for just a while."

"I will keep working." Julian said. "You will be at the rock?" he asked, knowing that Josh often walked out to the rock in the desert to think.

"I will be at the rock." Josh nodded, "If you need me."

"We will find her, Josh." Julian said, his voice sounding more confident than he felt.

Josh left the room and Julian retreated to his own office. There he turned on the video camera hidden in the bushes and rocks of the desert where Josh would be walking. He no longer trusted anyone but himself to keep Josh alive.

***

As she ate, Payton attempted small talk, anything to keep her from asking questions herself.

"The baby must be really close." Payton said.

"The doctor says another week, tops." Maria replied taking another bite of cheese.

"Amelia just discovered she was pregnant also." Payton said with a smile, " Our children will be able to play with one another."

"Mumm," Maria said, "That will be nice. I thought that might be the case when she called last week. She was so full of questions. Congratulations, Payton."

"Do you plan to return to work? I know Andrew valued your mind at Crytech."

"No, at least not for years. It is full time motherhood for me."

"I think Amelia is already looking at nannies," Payton said, still smiling, "Then again, she is not as together as you are. I am sure she will need help."

181

"She may surprise you, Payton." Maria said absently. "How much longer?"

Payton looked down at his watch, "We should be on the ground in another ten minutes or so."

He watched as she turned and looked out the window, he could see the concern in her face. He suppressed a smile when he realized that she totally trusted him, she had no idea of what she was about to face.

Chapter Thirty One

Maria was thankful that Payton had been so kind to her on this trip. While she was worried about Josh, since she had no way of knowing what exactly was wrong, she had tried not to allow her concern to overwhelm her.

Even more, she worried about the stress of the trip on the baby. For the last hour or so, she wondered if the trip would bring on labor. As much as she wanted the child to make her entrance into the world, she did not want it to happen at forty thousand feet, nor did she want her born in a country so far from home.

'Whatever will be, will be.' she told herself silently. She had noticed that of late she had begun using many of the speech expressions that she had heard her adoptive parents use throughout her life.

She was so lost in thought, she had not noticed that the plane had begun its descent. Only when the wheels touched down was she aware that she had returned to earth. Looking out the window, she was surprised to see that they had landed at a private air strip instead of the Israeli International Airport. No wonder Payton had said she would not need a passport.

As the jet taxied to the end of the runway, she saw a black limousine pulling alongside. As soon as the plane had stopped, Payton jumped up and opened the cockpit door, not waiting for the pilot to do it for him.

He helped Maria down the stairs to the ground below. On the ground, Payton dismissed the limo driver, saying he preferred to drive himself. Maria though his actions strange, but did not question. Instead, she insisted on sitting up front with him, refusing to be chauffeured by him.

Payton drove the large automobile like he was used to big vehicles. She was impressed by the way he maneuvered the car on the one lane road through the desert. Moments later, he pulled the car through massive wrought iron gates that had opened when he pressed a button on the dash.

"What is this place?" Maria asked as she tried to take in everything she saw. The building in front of her was elaborately architected to appear to encompass the entire side of the mountain. The strong lines of glass and steel were radiantly lit by light she could not see. As Payton pulled up to the front of the building, she could see that in front of the building was a circular courtyard. From her vantage point inside the car, the entire foundation of the courtyard and building was made of highly polished marble.

Again, she asked, "What is this place, Payton? Where are we?"

Payton glared at her, all softness now gone from his eyes and face. "We are at ENKI Headquarters, my dear. This is where you will learn everything your husband has always tried to hide from you."

Maria was confused. She had heard of ENKI, yes, and knew that Josh was a board member. Yet she had no idea of what he did, having always assumed it was a charitable organization of some kind. She knew that the last building had been bombed more than two years earlier and that all members of the ENKI board had died, including Josh's father.

She turned back to Payton and found herself looking at the barrel of a small gun he held in his hand.

"Payton... " she began.

"Shut up." He said as he turned off the ignition of the car. "You know Maria, I thought you were smart. You really disappointed me."

184

"I do not understand... " she said, her fear for herself and her child growing as she looked into his eyes. 'He is mad.' she thought, 'What the hell am I going to do.'

"There are so many things you do not understand, my dear. But I will educate you before you die." Payton said.

"Why? Why, Payton?

"The why is the easiest answer of all, my dear. That child you carry can never be born."

Maria could not stop the tears from running down her face. Looking at Payton, she realized he meant every word he was saying. All she could do was stall for time, maybe someone would come, she prayed silently.

"Explain it to me, Payton. Please explain it to me." she pleaded.

Payton laughed. "Like I said, Maria, I thought you were smart. I planted those seeds in your lab. I thought you were smart enough to figure out what they were, but I was wrong."

"The seeds?" Maria asked, "The apple seeds? What... "

"They have everything to do with this." Payton spat at her. "Get out of the car, I will explain as we go inside."

Maria opened the car door and swung her feet outside. She looked around as she pulled herself out of the car, hoping to see somewhere to run--but saw nothing. Payton slid across the seat and stepped out behind her, putting the gun in her back, pushing her forward to the front doors of the building.

As they crossed the courtyard, Maria could tell that the marble was inlaid with color, each different making the shape of a thirteen pointed star.

Behind her, Payton began to speak.

"Those seeds were developed by your husband, Maria. By his father really, but refined by Josh. Those seeds cause sterility in the children of those that eat them. That was Josh's plan for the world. Breed out the poor and hungry and leave a world of no one but those he desired to have."

"I do not believe you." Maria said, "Josh would not do that."

"Maria, dear, you have to understand who Josh is... who we all are. Turn around." he said, grabbing her by the arm.

"See that star? That is who we are. The thirteen. For generation after generation we have been together. Do you not find it strange that none of us have friends other than each other? We have been forced since childhood to work together, to learn together. None of us were raised with brothers or sisters. All of our fathers are dead. They all died together. Do you not find that strange?"

Maria started to speak, but thought better of it. Just let him talk, buy time.

"Do you know why it is so damn important that the child in your belly is a boy?" he asked.

Maria shook her head.

"Because he is the chosen one for the next generation. You will never be allowed another child, Maria. There can be only one child born to the Christianson line."

"But what if it had been a girl?" Not wanting to believe what he was saying, but she had to ask.

"The child would have been taken by an adoption agency. You would have been told it was dead."

"Josh would not have done that to me. He loves me." Maria realized her voice sounded desperate.

"He would, just as every generation before him has. Just like your own father did you, in order to have the chosen son."

"My own father? What do you know about my father?"

"I know everything about you, Maria. So does Josh and so does your brother Julian."

Maria's breath caught in her throat. "Julian.." her voice trailed off.

"Yes, Maria, my sweet. Julian is your half-brother. Do you never notice the resemblance between the two of you. Did you never wonder why in school he stopped perusing you?"

"I don't believe that..."

"Believe it my dear, you have so much to learn."

They had arrived at the doors of the building, still pointing the gun at her, Payton reached around and opened one of the doors.

"Inside, my dear."

Inside the building, the star was again repeated on the floor of the main entrance. A large marble spiral staircase led upward from the stars center.

"Payton, please. I have got to rest. Can I please sit? For just a moment?"

A comical look came across Payton's face. He shrugged his shoulders, "Sure sit for a spell."

Maria lowered her body into one of the oversized chairs against the wall. Looking around the room, she saw several security cameras. She looked back at Payton who was staring at her with cold blank eyes.

"Josh is not here, is he?" she asked, fearful of the answer.

"No one is here, Maria. It is just you and I."

"Why are you doing this Payton?"

"I told you. I have to do to Josh what he has done to me."

"Done to you?" she stammered.

"He has destroyed me. Do you not understand? I can never carry on the line of the thirteen and it is his fault. His fault."

"I don't..."

"I ate the god dammed apples, don't you get it? The thirteen dies with me. Amelia's child is not mine - it belongs to some museum curator." Payton was screaming now.

"But Payton, you could still have a child."

He laughed, "But what good would it do, the child would be sterile."

The sound filled Maria with dread. She looked wildly about, looking for somewhere to escape the madman that Payton had become.

In a calm voice, Payton asked, "Do not you want to know who the thirteen are, Maria? Are you not curious?"

She did not know how to answer the question, so she remained silent. He began screaming,

"You have to know, before you die, just how important this child is that you carry."

Again, she looked around the large room, she saw a shadow move just above her on the staircase. Payton was still looking at her, as she saw Julian rise up above the banister, holding his fingers to his lips.

Waving the gun at her again, Payton said, "Enough rest. Come on, upstairs. It is time you knew it all."

She pushed herself to her feet. Julian had disappeared, but now she held hope that she and her child might live. Walking slowly, she made her way to the bottom of the staircase and took the first step up into the unknown.

The steps were steep and she had to use the banister to help pull herself up each one. Payton was right behind her, urging her upward.

"Just think Maria, my dear. You are about to learn what no woman has ever known in two millennium."

Maria tried to think of something to say, to keep him talking. Her mind confused with everything he had told her, she finally asked,

"Tell me more about the thirteen, Payton. How can I be Julian's sister?"

Payton laughed gleefully behind her, "You and Julian share the same father, Patrick Benedict. Your mothers were twin sisters."

"He had two wives?" she asked.

"Did you never try to find your parents, Maria? You knew you were adopted."

"I tried for many years," she replied, "I could never find out anything."

She paused on the steps to catch her breath, it looked as if there were at least ten more before reaching the landing ahead. She looked back at Payton, who with wild eyes, appeared happy to be telling her everything.

"You mother died the day she gave birth to you." Payton paused, "No you did not kill her. She had had a wreck in the Swiss Alps -- went flying off the side of a mountain. Patrick Benedict was enraged when he found out you were a girl. He left the hospital and never went back. He deserted you, Maria as you were not the precious boy child he expected. He married Alicia's sister, three months later. Was not long before Julian was born and all was right in Patrick Benedict's world."

Maria looked in ahead of her, hoping to catch sight of Julian again, almost afraid that he had been a figment of her imagination. She saw no sign of him or anyone else. She felt the gun barrel in her back, as Payton forced her onwards.

"Tell me about Josh." she said, still hoping that if she kept him talking it would be easier to get away.

Behind her, Payton snorted. "Your beloved Josh. Do you know how little he cares about you Maria?"

"Tell me." she said.

"Did you know he maintains homes and flats all around the globe? Did you know that many times he has told you he is away on business -- he is really away at one of these places, picking up strange women and bedding them?"

Once again, Maria did not know how to answer, so remained silent. Her heart wanted to believe that Josh had been faithful to her, but her head heard a ring of truth in the words Payton said.

"He is the supreme son of the thirteen," Payton continued, "he can do no wrong. The others always agree with him. No matter what. Did you know we all had to swear allegiance to him, with a dagger at our throat, when took control of the ENKI table?" Payton began laughing again. "Here is one more for you Maria, my sweet. Did you know that your beloved Josh and your brother Julian are the ones that plotted their own father's murder."

"No... " the word escaped Maria's lips almost as a whisper.

"They planned the bombing, everything." Payton's voice sounded arrogant, hostile. His next sentence sounded proud, "We, each of us, slit our own father's throat."

They had reached the landing and he propelled her toward double wooden doors at the end of the short hallway.

"Inside this room, you will find I have told you nothing but truth, my dear lady. And then you will die."

Payton reached around her and opened the door. Inside the room, she saw the massive table surrounded by thirteen chairs. In the center of the star on the table, stood what appeared to be an ancient book, several inches thick, resting open on a small podium. Payton pushed her inside.

"There -- the book -- go read it." He said following her into the room.

Feeling compelled, Maria walked toward the book, while Payton remained standing just inside the door.

"Take the book, Maria. Sit down in your beloved's chair. Read and learn just who your husband is.

From behind her, Maria heard a sound, she turned to see Julian struggling with Payton. She ran as fast as she could to the other side of the table, and ducked, afraid the gun would go off.

Julian wrestled Payton out into the hallway.

"You can not stop me." she heard Payton say.

Unable to help herself, she rose and walked to the door to watch. Julian, although bigger and heavier than, Payton, had difficulty slowing the rage of the younger man. They reached the top of the landing, before Julian dealt the blow that sent Payton rolling down the staircase.

Maria began walking toward the landing, stopping only when Julian lifted his hand. Coming back to where she stood, he led her back to the boardroom.

"This is not over yet, Maria. Stay here. I will lock the door. He will not be able to get in, no matter what happens out there."

As quickly as that was said, he was out the door pulling it closed behind him. She heard the cylinders click and then the sound of his footfalls as he ran back to the stair.

Maria walked to the window. Looking out over the courtyard, she saw a figure approaching the gates. It was Josh.

Maria did not know what to believe any longer. She did not know if she was any safer with Josh than she had been with Payton. She watched Josh cross the star of the courtyard.

Even with the doors and windows closed, Maria could hear the yelling that was happening below. As she watched from the window, she saw Payton rush from the building toward Josh.

Reaching up she unlatched the window, allowing it to swing open. Josh held open his arms toward Payton.

"Payton, my brother. No harm has been done. We can fix everything."

Payton looked puzzled, "Not everything." he said as he emptied the guns clip into Josh's chest.

Josh fell perfectly across the star, his feet together, his arms outstretched. Payton was babbling, his madness now totally taking control of the man. He fell to his knees, lifting his arms upward.

"I have killed Jesus Christ," he yelled to the heavens, "he can never live again."

Maria looked down at Payton and her dead husband. She did not know what to feel. Loss surely, but little else. She walked over and picked up the book. Had Payton told the truth? Holding the book in the crook of her arm, she looked again down on the scene below. In the distance, she could hear sirens approaching. She wondered if Julian was dead also.

She watched as Payton turned to stare upward at the window where she stood. She smiled. The sirens were louder now, she had nothing to fear. From behind her, she heard the door open and she turned her head to watch Julian enter the room and come to stand beside her.

Together they watched as the courtyard filled with police cruisers and handcuffs were placed on Payton.

"Your son is safe now." Julian said quietly. "I will protect him with my life."

"Will you Julian?"

"I have sworn to protect Josh's child."

Maria knew at that moment that much of what Payton had told her was truth. They watched as Payton was led away by the authorities below.

"I am sure you will be a good uncle to my daughter, Julian." she said.

"A girl child?"

"The only child. The only future." she said.

www.ingramcontent.com/pod-product-compliance
Lightning Source LLC
Chambersburg PA
CBHW070828180626
46818CB00001B/432